Sexfight Diary

Ian Faber

Published by Ian Faber, 2023.

SEXFIGHT DIARY

First edition. February 25, 2023.

Copyright © 2023 Ian Faber.

ISBN: 979-8215089231

Written by Ian Faber.

Also by Ian Faber

17th Century Sexfighters
A Dangerous Journey
Friendships Rekindled
The Female Island
True Freedom

21st Century Sexfighters
Porn Stars Reading Lines
Popular Porn Stars

Erotic Combat World Championship
Erika's First Sexfight
Ulrike, the Sexfighting Student

Good Friends, Better Lover
A New Opportunity
Workplace Sexfights

Standalone

Sexfight Diary

Table of Contents

Chapter 1 – Moving In 1

Chapter 2 – The Flirting Game 10

Chapter 3 – Movie Night 15

Chapter 4 – A Cultural Outing 20

Chapter 5 - Poker 25

Chapter 6 – The Shopping Spree 36

Chapter 7 – Slutty When Wet 46

Chapter 8 – The Duel at Dawn 60

Chapter 9 – A Change of Weapons 70

Chapter 10 – Pussy War 77

Chapter 11 – Tongues versus Clits 83

Chapter 12 – The Pussy Fighting Queen 85

Chapter 1 – Moving In

After placing the flower arrangement on the table, Stacy gave her spare room a last inspection to ensure everything was just right. Her best friend's daughter, Celeste, wasmoving in with her the next day. Her rental contract was comeing to an end and it would be approximately three months before she could move into the new apartment. The new development was being built only a few blocks away from Stacy's upmarket home. She could not wait to have some company in her huge house. She only saw her children, who were living far from home, once a year. Her son, Simon, was enlisted in the navy and stationed at a naval base in Hawaii. Her daughter, Emily, was studying a marine biology degree at the University of Miami. Holidays, except for the Christmas holidays, she worked at a small aquarium in Miami to gain practical experience

But Stacy had little time to long for her children. She had to prepare for a sexfight. Her husband, Gary, had been almost twenty years her senior. He had died from a heart attack ten years ago. When they were still married, sex with him was all she needed. He was a generous lover, as well as a good provider for her and their children. When he died, each of them inherited a significant sum of money. He had also left the house to Stacy and a chain of hardware stores for her and the children. Neither Stacy, nor the kids had any desire to be in the hardware business. With a competent management team in place, each of them earned significant dividends every six months.

After Gary's death, Stacy's sex life had been non-existent for a few months. But one day, while sorting out some of his stuff, she had found an old porn DVD they used to watch as part of their foreplay. It was a sexfight between two women, one in her forties and the other in her twenties. The clear rivalry between these two women always got her engine going. When she watched it again that day, she remembered how the two of them had fantasised about her being in a contest like this. These had only been fantasies, and neither of them ever wanted to make it a reality. But on that day when she watched it again, she decided to try sexfighting. Finding an opponent was tricky. It took her more than a month to track down another woman, who seemed sane, who also wanted to try a sexfight. They were both in their early thirties. Stacy was a widow, and her opponent Emily, who is Celeste's mother, was newly divorced.

1

The fight blew her mind. Her competitive juices, mixed in with pure lust, made her feel better than she had ever done before. The two women became best friends and sexfight opponents until Emily had moved to Canada for a job opportunity about two years ago.

After her first sexfight, Stacy was hooked. Many more followed, mostly against other women, but sometimes also against men. Her record against men was flawless, and although she had a few losses against women, she won most sexfights against female competitors. All her losses were against women around her age or older than her. She refused to lose to arrogant young sexfighters, no matter how horny they made her. Taming the up-and-coming sexfighters was her speciality. They would challenge her with a perfect record and leave with their tails between their legs and a blemished record.

Her fight tonight was against another young slut talking a big game, calling her too old to last, boasting about her own stamina and sexual prowess. These were the fights she enjoyed most. There were few things more satisfying than seeing the arrogance drain from a young slut's eyes while taking her to levels of ecstasy she had never experienced before.

Celeste wrapped her last ornament and placed it in a box marked for storage. Most of her furniture and other belongings would be held in storage for three months until the developers finished the new apartment building in which she purchased a flat. She was excited to move in with her mother's friend for a few months. Stacy had been part of her life since she was fifteen. After her parent's divorce, her father moved away and she almost never saw him. But her mother and Stacy visited each other regularly and she enjoyed having another strong female figure in her life. After her mother had moved to Canada, Celeste became closer with Stacy and they became good friends. Although they had a great relationship, their jobs kept them busy and she did not see Stacy as much as she wanted to. Celeste was a junior attorney at a big law firm, while the older woman was a director at an auditing firm. Both worked long hours, making it difficult to visit as often as they wanted to. This was why both of them had taken leave for two weeks to ensure they could spend lots of time together when Celeste moved in. It was not the best time to take leave for Stacy, as her firm was busy their biggest client with a large restructuring. But she convinced the office she needed some time off, and promised to be available when needed.

Thinking of her older friend, made Celeste miss her a lot. Although she was only supposed to move in the next day, she decided to surprise Stacy with an impromptu visit. After showering, she dressed in a short skirt and a thin blouse. The summer heat allowed her to show off her sexy twenty-five-year-old body. This was something she enjoyed doing. Having men and women forget what they were doing when she walked past, gave her a buzz. Her looks turned men's brains to mush and made women jealous. She enjoyed the jealousy almost more than the lust. As a competitive woman, she enjoyed having sexual contests with other women, whether these were virtual contests to see whether she could draw their men's attention on her, or actual sexfights. She had fought her first sexfight just over three years earlier. On a particularly hot summer's day, she had worn her sexiest one-piece swimsuit at a public swimming pool. It had a thong back and a zip in front, which she had zipped down all the way to her bellybutton, showing off ample amounts of firm C-cup breasts. A woman in her late thirties, whose husband could not keep his eyes off of her firm, young body, came over and whispered in Celeste's ear. At first, the young redhead thought the older woman wanted to beat her up when she whispered, 'I've beaten many young sluts like you.' But her intensions became clear when she continued. 'You may think men like your sexy, young body, but what they really want is good sex. I am much better at sex than you are, so if you do not want me to give you a sexfight lesson, go put something on.'

This intrigued Celeste. Although the woman was almost twice her age, she was very attractive. Back then, she had been with a few other women, but all around her own age. The thought of having sex with an older woman aroused her. The thought of having a sexual contest with an older woman made her extremely horny. 'I accept your challenge. Are you willing to fight for your husband? If I beat you, you have to watch while I have sex with him.' Although the younger woman had no genuine desire to sleep with the older guy, she knew no competitive woman could back out of the sexfight after such a challenge. Her instincts were right. The woman gave her a dirty look before turning to her husband. 'Frank, this one wants to join us in the Winnebago. Her husband grinned from ear-to-ear before grabbing their stuff. Ten minutes later, the two women were facing each other on the Winnebago's bed, while it was still parked in a busy parking lot. Although this was her first sexfight, Celeste made the older woman come so hard, she could only watch in silence while the young redhead rode her husband like a wild cowgirl. Humiliating this older woman the way she did, felt so good. Although she had many sexfights against women of her age and a few men, her speciality was to tame older women, especially those who were confident in their experience and therefore underestimating this young spitfire. Her record against older women was flawless, as she could not stand to lose to them and therefore pushed herself way further than she did against younger women and men.

When Stacy returned from another sexfight victory against an arrogant young slut, she found Celeste in her garden, flirting with the neighbour.

'Hi honey, I did not expect you tonight.' She gave the redhead a hug and a kiss on the cheek.

'I had a long day of packing and decided to surprise you.'

'What a pleasant surprise. I am starved. You can help me prepare dinner.'

'Thanks, aunt Stacy.'

'How many times must I tell you to drop the 'aunt'?'

'It sometimes just feels awkward to call you by your first name, especially when my mother is around.'

'Well, your mother is not around.'

'I know. I will make the effort.'

When they entered the house, Stacy put her keys in a bowl. 'Would you mind if I have a shower first? It's been a long day. Maybe you can open a nice bottle of wine in the meantime.'

'I will do better than that. I will start with dinner while you take a shower.'

'Great. There is a chicken in the fridge. I planned to cook it tonight.'

After showering, Stacy took a diary from the bedside table. She ran her fingers over the expensive leather cover before opening it to make some notes in it. She was just about done when Celeste popped her head into the room.

'Do you still have some of the nice Portuguese chicken spice?'

'Yes, there are some in the cupboard in the hall.'

'Thanks, what are you writing?'

'Just some notes in my diary.'

'I did not know you kept a diary. I hope you only write nice things about me.'

'It is not about you.'

'What is it about, then?'

'Don't be nosy.' Stacy closed the diary and placed it back in the bedside table drawer. She locked the drawer and put the key in her handbag before showing the young woman where the spice was. She was not sure whether the redhead would understand that she had sex with both men and women and that she enjoyed having sexfights. Although they had been open to each other about their sex lives during the last few years, neither had ever told the other that she had sex with women as well. As Stacy had been in sexfights with Celeste's mother, she kept this part of her life a secret from her young friend. Celeste believed that the brunette was old-fashioned about sex and that she would not understand why a woman would choose to have sex with men and women and why she would enjoy erotic contests with them. Both believed the other only had sex with men and neither had a clue that the other enjoyed competitive sex.

Two days later, after Celeste had moved in, Stacy had to pop into the office for a quick meeting with a client and to instruct her team on how to deal with the matter. When she was done, she phoned her young friend and asked her to pack her gym bag and to meet her at the gym for a session. After packing her own gym bag, Celeste went into the older woman's room to find her gym gear and to pack her bag. While doing this, she could not help but to wonder what the brunette had written in the diary two days earlier. At first, she resisted her urges to snoop, but when she saw the handbag in which the brunette had placed the key for the drawer, she just had to check whether the key was still inside. In her haste to get to the office, Stacy had grabbed the wrong handbag that morning, leaving the drawer key behind. Celeste found it after rummaging through the handbag. She sat down on the bed, wrestling with her conscience. Surely, she could not invade her friend's privacy. She almost put the key back in the handbag, but curiosity soon got the better of her. She looked towards the door to make sure nobody was watching her, although she knew she was home alone. Once satisfied that the coast was clear, she unlocked the drawer and took out the diary. She held it in her hands for a while, deciding whether to open it. Guilt was gnawing at her conscience, but she soon found a justification for having a look. *Female friends should share everything with each other. I have the right to read this, especially if she said something about me.'*

Once the diary was open, she paged to the last entry. It had the date and the name Phoebe next to it. The first paragraph had Phoebe's age and a brief description of her looks. The next paragraph was captioned 'Weaknesses'. In this paragraph, her mother wrote:

'Her nipples are extremely sensitive. I think I could give her a nipple orgasm in a future fight. Kissing her neck distracts her and makes her lose focus, especially when I give her gentle love bites.

The following paragraph was captioned 'Strengths.' She wrote:

'She is very sexy. I was worked up the moment she stripped naked. For her size, she is very strong and a good wrestler. She identified my weaknesses quickly and focussed on them.

The next paragraph had a detailed description of the positions used, the techniques used by each fighter, when she was close to an orgasm and when she thought her opponent was on the edge, and the techniques both used to avoid an orgasm

The last paragraph had the following in it:

'Another win against an arrogant young slut. My perfect record against women in their twenties continues.'

Celeste could not believe what she just read. Her friend had been in a sexfight the day she came over for a surprise visit. Stacy, a sexfighter? She was shocked, but not in a bad way. Sexfighting was just something she never associated with the older woman. She shook her head slowly, while a smile came over her face. 'Wow, who would ever guess?' She paged through the diary, quickly reading through account after account of the brunette's sexfights. It quickly became clear to her how much her older friend enjoyed taming younger sexfighters like herself. 'Have I found an older woman who might give me a proper challenge?' She had to say this out loud to make it real and not just some wild fantasy. But she almost immediately knew that this could never happen. 'I should not be thinking these thoughts about my mother's best friend,' she once again said out loud. But then she found an entry for Emily. *'Could this be my mother? Is this how they became friends?'* She found a few more entries for Emily. Some of them read *'My friend Emily'.* Celeste's mind was blown. She had just found out that her mother's best friend was a sexfighter. Now she knew that her mother was also a sexfighter and that the two of them had been in quite a few sexfights. Her emotions were all over the place. *'How did they keep it a secret from me. I can't believe my mother never won any of their sexfights. How good is Stacy. Would she be able to push me all the way?'* After carefully placing the diary back exactly the way she found it, she locked the drawer and placed the key back in the handbag before she grabbed their bags and headed for the gym. Her initial amazement had now turned into respect for Stacy and her mother and curiosity about her older friend's sexfights.

The gym was busy as usual. Stacy was already waiting at the juice bar when the redhead arrived. They gave each other a quick hug and a kiss on the cheek before heading for the change rooms to change. A few minutes later, they were on two adjacent treadmills to get their heart rates going. Celeste could not help herself. She had to glance at her the brunette's D-cups bouncing about, as if they tried to escape the confines of the small gym top covering them. With the knowledge she had gained earlier, she now saw the older woman in a different light. This very attractive body next to her was a sexfighting machine. She wondered how the women who had faced her friend felt when they pressed their breasts into those magnificent breasts. Her love for her older friend now lived hand-in-hand in her brain with respect and awe for the sexfighter she was. This was a woman who enjoyed beating younger women in sexfights. This was the kind of woman she spent countless hours searching for on the sexfighting forums. There was no greater satisfaction for her than to beat older women who underestimated younger sexfighters like herself. Knowing that the brunette had a flawless record against women in their twenties, made it impossible for her not to wonder whether she could beat her older friend in an erotic contest. But she pressed these thoughts aside and focussed on exercising for a while.

After fifteen minutes on the treadmills, the two women towelled down before moving to the resistance machines.

'You look so cute in that outfit, Stacy. Not many women can pull that off.' Although this was an innocent comment, Celeste immediately wondered whether the brunette would construe this as flirting. Now that she knew her friend was also into women, she was not sure where the line between innocent compliments and flirting was.

'Thank you, darling. I have to work very hard to keep my older body in shape, though.'

'That makes it even more impressive. You look better than most of the women in this gym.'

'You are too kind.' Although Stacy knew she was a beautiful woman, it felt very good to get such a compliment from a very sexy young woman. This made her feel great and put a smile on her face for most of their gym session.

When they were done, the two women headed to the change rooms for a shower. Celeste felt happy and wanted to share her joy with the older woman. Spreading her arms, she said, 'Thanks, Stacy. Working out with you was so much fun. I thought I could outwork you, but you are so competitive.'

The older woman gave her young friend a friendly smile before accepting her hug. 'I am competitive, aren't I? But you have always been competitive as well.'

Their sexy bodies pressed together while they hugged. The redhead did not hold the embrace for too long, but she was well aware that their ample breasts pressed tightly into each other. This made her nipples stiffen up. Stacy also enjoyed the tight hug with the redhead, but thought little about their breasts squashing together as this often happened when she hugged other women.

After they've both removed their clothes, Celeste looked at her own figure in the mirror to find any areas which still needed work. The brunette joined her to also searched for any imperfections. The younger woman could not control her curiosity. Her eyes kept wandering between the reflection of her own body and that of her friend's body.

The redhead was proud of her firm C-cup breasts and her long, pink nipples, but she absolutely adored her friend's, slightly droopy D-cups and her thick brown nipples. Both sets of breasts towered over flat tummies and clean-shaven pussies. Celeste kept her red hair in a pixy cut, while the older woman's black hair was cut shoulder-length. Both had high cheekbones, thin noses and full lips. The redhead had emerald green eyes, while the brunette had brown eyes. The older woman had a 38 – 29 – 38 figure, was about five-foot-six-inches tall and weighed a hundred-and-twenty-five pounds. The stunning twenty-five-year-old was also five-foot-six-inches tall and weighed a hundred-and-fifteen pounds with measurements of 36 – 28 – 36. They both had tight bums and athletic legs, with silky smooth skins.

After inspecting their bodies, the two women showered in adjacent showers. Celeste glanced over at her forty-three-year-old naked friend a few times but did not make any comments and did not touch the brunette's body.

She felt slightly embarrassed for having the urge to stare at her friend's beautiful naked body, and she did not want her friend to catch her doing so.

Chapter 2 – The Flirting Game

After dinner that night, the two women shared a bottle of wine while talking about plans for their two week holiday together. The knowledge that her friend was also a sexfighter still distracted Celeste, but she hid this well from the brunette.

'Are you still having judo lessons at the same dojo, Stacy?' This thought came out of the blue as, moments before, they had been talking about going to an art exhibition.

'Yes, but I only attend classes once a week now.'

'Is that hunk still the Sensei?'

'Jean-Pierre? Yes, he is still there.'

'Maybe I should join you for your next lesson. I have not been to a Dojo since Eric and I broke up three months ago. I could not go back to his Dojo after that and I have not found another one yet.' Eric was Celeste's last boyfriend. She had been single for the last three months and did not have nearly enough sex during this time.

'I think you just want to perve on Jean-Pierre,' said the brunette in a teasing way.

'Now you're going to pretend you don't go to the Dojo to perve on him?' The younger woman also said this in a teasing manner.

'Who doesn't? Anyway, I need some eye candy after James moved on to one of his many sluts.' Stacy broke up with her last boyfriend about four months earlier, after he had accidentally sent her a message meant for a woman he was seeing on the side. 'A girl needs to do what a girl needs to do.'

They both laughed, before Celeste almost asked her friend about her sexfighting career, but thankfully managed to stop herself.

'Maybe we can go this Friday, but only if you promise not to embarrass me. I would like to be welcome there for the foreseeable future.'

'I promise not to perve on him too hard.' They laughed again before the redhead continued. 'It is my bedtime. The gym session took a lot out of me.'

'I need to go to bed as well. We need to be at the market early tomorrow to ensure we get the prettiest flowers.' She motioned with her head towards the arrangement on a table. 'These ones need to be replaced.'

10

'I look forward to that.'

They got up and gave each other a long hug. Celeste, once again, enjoyed the feeling of her friend's breasts pressing into hers. Like earlier that day, her nipples jumped to attention. This time, she could feel the brunette's large nipples brushing against hers just before they broke their hug.

When Celeste got to her room, she gently squeezed her breasts before running her fingers over her erect nipples. She was very horny and knew she would have to take care of herself. After stripping naked, she lay down on her bed, trying to imagine Jean-Pierre without a shirt on, but the only images flashing in her brain were of her older friend tribbing with another woman. At first, she tried to force these from her mind, but the hotter she got from rubbing her clit, the clearer these images became. By the time an orgasm washed through her body, she imagined it was Stacy forcing her to come. She both loved this idea and hated it. The thought of having a sexfight against Stacy excited her very much, but the idea of losing to her angered her. She hated losing sexfights and could not take the idea of losing to an older woman. Her hands slowly brushed over her body until they found her breasts. She squeezed them gently, while thinking of her friend again.

But her conscience quickly interfered with her fantasy. This felt wrong. After a deep sigh, she got up and put her sexy silk pyjamas on. These felt so sensual against her skin and she was soon massaging her breasts again. As soon as she did so, her mind pictured the brunette being fingered by another woman. She fought against these thoughts for a bit, but then decided to just enjoy them. Fantasies and thoughts hurt nobody. There could be no harm in picturing her friend in a sexfight while playing with herself.

She continued squeezing her breasts while thumbing her nipples through the thin material of the tight top. This made her nipples even harder than they already had been. While doing this, she imagined it was Stacy massaging her breasts. This made her pussy soaking wet with lust. She quickly removed her top, allowing her fingers to feel the bare skin of her breasts and to stroke her stiff nipples, which were buzzing with pure joy.

As her right hand slowly glided downwards over her silky skin, her clit grew hard in anticipation of the attention it was about to get. The redhead closed her eyes and suddenly it was her older friend's fingers gliding under her silk shorts until it found her throbbing clit. She imagined doing the same to the brunette, while her fingers rubbed her erect clit faster and faster until her whole body exploded with wave after wave of pleasure. When she eventually opened her eyes after riding out the mighty orgasm and all its aftershocks, it surprised her to find her older friend was not on the bed with her. It had felt so real. It had felt so good.

Mixed feelings of guilt and excitement kept her awake for hours. At first, she rolled around, trying to focus her mind on something else so she could fall asleep. Eventually, she reached over and grabbed a magazine from her nightstand. Paging through it, she found an article with tips for women on how to pleasure themself. She sighed before following the instructions. This immediately brought a fantasy of her and her older friend having a sexfight back into her mind. A tremendous orgasm soon rocked her body again. She was not sure whether this was because of the tips in the magazine or the fantasy of having a sexfight with the brunette, but she did not care. She was in seventh heaven.

The next morning, Celeste was still very sleepy when her friend brought her coffee in bed.

'You look like you had a rough night. Is the mattress comfortable enough? Are the pillows too hard or too soft?'

'They are all fine. I think the wine just went to my head. I will be okay after this coffee and a nice hot shower.' The redhead wondered whether her friend could see in her eyes what she had been fantasising about the previous night. Although she was no longer feeling the guilt which had bothered her the previous night, she was still not comfortable with the idea of the brunette finding out about her fantasies.

After having her coffee, Celeste stripped down and jumped into the shower. The moment her hands touched her wet body, the images of her older friend sexfighting a young woman flashed into her mind again. This time, she did not try to ignore them. Instead, she gave her clit a good hard rubbing until her legs turned to jelly while a powerful orgasm rolled through her body.

'I have to sexfight her,' she thought. This was suddenly very clear to her. She needed to know who the best sexfighter between them was. She needed to know whether her friend's winning streak against young women would continue, or whether she could keep her flawless record against older women. But how could she establish whether Stacy would be interested in a sexfight against her without potentially making things between them very awkward? *'Maybe I should flirt with her. If she flirts back, I can push it further. If the flirting makes her uncomfortable, I can always say I was just giving her a compliment, or even that I was just having some harmless fun.'*

By the time the redhead joined the brunette in the kitchen for breakfast, she was fully committed to her plan of flirting with the older woman in order to establish whether she was up for a sexfight. She also believed that flirting may arouse her sexy older friend to a point where she was ready for a sexfight, even if she was not already at that point. Although the potential of a sexfight with her friend excited her, she knew that rushing it may ruin her chances. She had to start slowly and build up from there. If she did this correctly, the brunette would not even realise she was building her up.

After breakfast, the two women headed for the market. It was still early and there were only a few other vehicles on the road. They therefore made it to the market, while most of the vendors were still unpacking their merchandise. Stacy headed directly to her favourite flower shop. Once there, she picked out a selection of flowers for the living room.

'These are so lovely, and they last long.' The brunette removed a carnation from its bucket and smelled it before moving it to her young friend's nose so she could smell it as well.

'They are beautiful, but not nearly as pretty as you, Stacy.' The younger woman caressed her friend's arm while saying this. She had a sweet smile on her face and ensured she made eye contact with the older woman.

'Thank you, darling.' The brunette loved compliments about her looks. Getting a compliment from such a sexy young woman this early in the morning, brightened up her day. She returned the smile before landing a quick kiss on the redhead's cheek. 'Just because you are so nice to me, you can pick flowers for your room as well.'

'Thank you. I will pick only the prettiest flowers to remind me of you when I wake up every morning.' Celeste kissed her friend on the cheek, close to her lips before giving her a tight hug, ensuring that their large breasts pressed into each other. She held the embrace longer than she normally would, moving her upper body slightly to rub her hard nipples over the older woman's nipples.

'You are welcome, honey.' Stacy enjoyed the hug. It always felt so good to hold her sexy friend close to her. Making the younger woman happy was very rewarding. Although she felt the redhead's nipples brush over hers, she thought little of this. The fact that her own nipples woke up from this was no surprise to her. They had always been very sensitive and reacted to the slightest touch or when her breasts were massaged or squeezed by another woman's breasts. Her friend's firm breasts did a good job of pressing hers, but this often happened when women with large breasts hugged each other, so she did not suspect that this was done on purpose.

When they broke their hug, Celeste gave the older woman another kiss on the cheek, this time even closer to her mouth. 'You give the best hugs, Stacy. I can hug you for hours.'

'I love hugging you too, honey.'

Celeste was slightly disappointed that her friend had not recognised their nipple rub as a challenge for a sexfight. But she was satisfied that her flirting was not too obvious, but still had given the brunette some joy. It was a good start and she was hopeful her efforts would bear fruit soon.

Stacy felt good. This outing with the redhead was very pleasant and the compliments and affection lifted her spirits and made her feel positive about herself and life in general.

Chapter 3 – Movie Night

That evening, Celeste suggested that the two of them should watch a movie. She had thought long and hard before picking a romantic drama which had enough sad scenes, romantic scenes and even a raunchy sex scene during which the lead actress bared her breasts. She made popcorn and placed a box of tissues on the table next to her friend's side of the couch before fetching a bottle of wine and two glasses. When everything was ready, she bounced back to her room to put on her lace pyjamas, with no underwear. She knew the brunette also did not wear a bra under her satin nightie, so she suggested that the older woman should also change to her sleepwear just in case they fell asleep on the couch. This suggestion made sense to the Stacy, so she also went to her room to slip into her very comfortable satin nighty.

As soon as the two women sat down on the couch next to each other, Celeste started the movie. After a few minutes, she moved closer and leaned over her friend, reaching for the popcorn. This caused her left breast to press into the brunette's right breast. With only thin material covering their breasts, both women could clearly feel the other's nipple brushing over hers, making both these nipples stand proudly. Celeste purposefully fumbled with the popcorn for a while, ensuring that their breasts pressed together for almost ten seconds.

At first, Stacy felt slightly awkward, but she knew the new generation was much more comfortable with other women touching their breasts than her generation had been when they were in their twenties. She had witnessed women allowing others to feel their breasts in the change rooms of the gym. Normally this started with one of them telling the other how firm her breasts looked. Inevitably, the answer was something like, 'Thank you. Do you want to feel them?' After the woman who paid the compliment had fondled the other's breasts for a while, she would usually say something like, 'I wish mine were that firm. Just feel them.' The other would then fondle her breasts before assuring her they were also nice and firm.

Then there was the breast-bump. While young men fist-bumped each other after a rewarding workout, some of the young women would bump their breasts into each other. Although Stacy would probably never breast-bump another

15

woman, or invite her to fondle her breasts, unless they were having sex or a sexfight, she respected the younger generation for being so comfortable with their bodies. She assumed her friend was just being young and carefree about where she placed her breasts and, therefore, read nothing into their very enjoyable breast encounter.

The movie started with a happy couple, but soon turned sad when the boyfriend suddenly disappeared. When this happened, the redhead snuggled up to the brunette and rested her head on the older woman's shoulder, ensuring that her warm breath occasionally blew on her friend's neck.

Having her young friend snuggle up to her during the sad scenes comforted Stacy. She turned her head and gave the redhead a tender kiss on the forehead before returning her focus to the movie. But soon the warm breath on her neck made her shiver with delight. Both her nipples were now hard. She felt slightly awkward for being turned on by her friend's breath and considered moving away from her. But she told herself she was being silly and that it is only natural to get turned on by hot breath on her neck, no matter whose breath it was. This was especially true, as she had not been intimate with anybody for over a month. She had some sexfights, but there was little time for intimacy during competitive sex.

Seeing how hard her friend's nipples were, Celeste took her flirting to the next level. Her hand searched until it found the older woman's hand. When it did, she slid her fingers between the brunette's fingers, the way sexfighters sometimes showed their desire to have a tribbing sexfight with each other. She hoped that her older friend would recognise this challenge and react to it positively.

When the redhead intertwined their fingers, it brought back many memories for Stacy. She vividly remembered how a colleague's wife had challenged her to a sexfight a few months earlier. They were at a work function when their eyes locked. Both could see the competitiveness in the other's eyes and immediately suspected the other might also be into sexfights. When they both went for a fresh drink, her colleague's wife took her hand and intertwined their fingers while moving her hand slightly, mimicking the movement during a tribbing sexfight. Stacy accepted the challenge by using her fingers to return the rubbing. This sealed the deal. A few minutes later, Stacy's queen size bed creaked, as if it was ready to break, as the pussies of the two horny women battled with one another in a steamy sexfight in her hotel room. It was one of the wilder and more competitive sexfights Stacy had ever had. Thinking about it, the brunette still wondered if their loud moans and their trash talking had been heard outside of the hotel room that day.

But the brunette did not suspect for a moment that her her young friend knew anything about sexfight challenges. She therefore enjoyed the handholding as mere affection shared by two friends. Both of them snuggled closer to the other while the lead actress was pushed towards her breaking point while figuring out what happened to her boyfriend.

This caused their side-boobs to press into each other. Although Celeste had not planned this, she made the most of it, moving about as if she was trying to get more comfortable. This caused their side-boobs to rub into each other.

Stacy did not take too much notice of this. Her focus was mainly on the movie. Although she enjoyed the feeling of their breasts rubbing into each other, she did not suspect her friend of any deliberate rubbing.

Towards the end of the movie, after the lead actress reunited with her boyfriend, the sex scene started. After they kissed for a while, the lead actress pushed her boyfriend onto the bed before giving him a slow striptease. With every piece of clothing she removed, she used her hand to sensually touch her own body.

This made both women on the couch wet with lust. The redhead used her older friend's focus on the scene to subtly move her leg until their naked thighs brushed against each other.

Electric pulses raced to their brains the moment their silky skins touched. Stacy was concerned her yung friend might see just how much this aroused her. She thought about moving her leg away, but she could not get herself to stop the magical feeling their thighs shared.

When the lead actress tossed her bra on the floor to expose her firm D-cups, Stacy commented on them. 'She has such magnificent breasts.'

Celeste immediately paused the movies to give them a chance to discuss the actress' naked breasts. 'They are gorgeous, but I don't think they are as nice as yours.'

This made the older woman blush. 'You think I have nice breasts?'

'You have the perfect breasts. They are big, firm, beautifully shaped and your nipples are ten times nicer than hers.'

'Thank you, darling. You have very beautiful breasts as well.'

'Thanks. They are smaller than yours, though.'

The compliment about her breasts made the brunette feel very good about herself. She had always been proud of them, but it was very nice to realise just how much her sexy young friend appreciated them. Nipples was not something she would discuss often, but the door was open, so she walked right through it.

'Her only flaw is probably her lack of nipples. One can hardly see whether they are erect. I have always enjoyed the sight of a long, thick nipple.'

'So have I. Luckily, the two of us have been blessed with proper nipples. I often get looks from strangers because of my nipples poking through a blouse. I am sure you have the same issue.'

'Yes, it is not always easy to hide these.'

Both women smiled while glancing over at the other's hard nipples. Both were very horny from watching the sex scene, which was now in full swing after Celeste had un-paused the movie. The actress was now riding the actor, after removing his clothes as well. Her magnificent breasts were heaving up and down on her chest, while soft moans escaped her mouth.

At the end of the movie, both women urgently needed sexual relief. Celeste realised that her older friend was not yet ready to cross the sexual line with her, so she faked a yawn to signal it was time to go to bed.

Stacy did not realise how much the redhead had been flirting with her. The thought of having sex with the younger woman had not even entered her mind. All she thought about was how to get to her room as soon as possible without making it obvious that she needed to touch herself. When her young friend yawned, she took the hint.

'I am also exhausted. I think I will have an early night.'

'That is a good idea. It has been a long day.'

After agreeing it was bedtime, the two women got up before hugging and kissing. The hug just made them hornier when their breasts pressed together and their hard nipples jousted for a split second. The brunette quickly separated from her hot friend and said good night, giving her a tender light kiss on the cheek.

That night, each of them pleasured themselves to multiple orgasms. This made Celeste even more determined to have a sexfight with her friend.

However, Stacy blamed her lust on the movie, although deep down, she knew the younger woman also contributed to her arousal.

Chapter 4 – A Cultural Outing

The next day, the two women had a relaxing day at home until Stacy paged through the cultural portion of the local newspaper and saw there was an exhibition of one of her favourite artist's artwork.

'Come look at this. Nancy Le Roux is exhibiting at the Artzone.'

'Who is she?'

'A very talented young artist. I love her work and have always wanted to buy a few pieces. Maybe I will find a few today. You will also love her once you see her work.'

'It sounds like fun. Do you want to go?' Although Celeste enjoyed a pretty picture, she was not that much into art. But she knew how much her older friend enjoyed viewing art pieces, so she was keen to go.

'Yes. Maybe you will find something for your new apartment as well.'

'Maybe I will, but let's focus on getting you some new art.'

Forty minutes later, the two women arrived at the Artzone. It was a small, privately owned gallery in a neighbourhood where many up-and-coming artists lived. Stacy loved to visit it as there was always a chance of purchasing an early work of the next artist making it big. But the reason she purchased art was not only for a potential investment, she was also passionate about supporting local artists.

When they entered the gallery, a few beautiful landscape paintings drew Celeste's attention, but her friend headed straight towards the small exhibition room. The redhead followed the older woman, but was truly disappointed when they entered the room. She had never been a fan of abstract art and all the pieces in the exhibition room were abstract. The older woman was in seventh heaven, though. She hurried from one piece to another with a huge smile on her face. Just when Celeste thought the brunette had viewed all the paintings, she went back to the first one to study it properly.

'Don't you just love this?'

'I do not understand abstract art. All I see in this one is a very nice boob.'

'Don't be silly.' Stacy knew her young friend did not enjoy this kind of art and also knew that she was using humour to entertain herself. She smiled before continuing. 'I see the struggle everyone has to navigate through the light and dark sides of their personalities.'

'I still see a very nice boob with a magnificent nipple. Were you the model for this one?'

A couple looked around with judgement written all over their faces when Stacy burst out laughing. She lifted her hand to apologise for disturbing the subdued atmosphere. She knew this would not be the last time her young friend would make her laugh. The redhead had that naughty expression on her face, which always led to lots of fun. They moved on to the next painting.

'Dare I ask what you think about this one?'

'Well, I thought it was obvious. It depicts the joys of a madam in a Dutch brothel while pleasuring herself after a long day of selling sex.'

The couple looked around again when the brunette burst into laughter. This time, the couple shook their heads before leaving the exhibition room.

'You ruined their experience. Please stop making me laugh.'

'I did everybody a favour. Their attitude stinks. Surely people should be allowed to have fun while viewing art. There is no need for a stuffy atmosphere.'

'Well, I am indeed having fun.'

Celeste kept commenting on the paintings and the brunette kept laughing at her young friend for seeing something sexual in each of them. She was having a great time, while still seriously considering which pieces to purchase. It was telling that the redhead was focusing this much on sex. Stacy wondered whether she had been without a man for too long after breaking up with her boyfriend.

'This one is about two naked women wrestling for position before settling a dispute with a sexfight.' Celeste wondered whether she went too far with this. So far, she had entertained her friend, but would mentioning sexfights make things awkward between them?

'Mmm, interesting take.' Stacy laughed again, hiding her inner thoughts from the younger woman. But her mind was rushing with thoughts. *Does she know about my sexfights? How could she? Maybe she is a sexfighter as well? No, she does not even like women, she is only into men. It must be the internet. With all the information available, young people know about many things I only learned about later in life.'*

After viewing all the paintings. Stacy bought two, notably the *'breast'* and 'the *'sexfight'* paintings. Although she reassured herself that these were the two best paintings and that her young friend's comments did not influence her choice, there was a slight doubt creeping into her mind. Was Celeste just being funny, or had she deliberately been talking about sex with her today? Had she been flirting with her the last few days? Surely this was not the case. Surely, this was just how the younger generation interacted nowadays. But this was the first time she could recall the redhead being so flirty with her. Maybe something was indeed going on.

When they got home, Stacy placed the paintings on a table next to each other.

'You can pick one for your room. The other will go into my room.'

'Oh, this is a tough choice. Your lovely breast, or two naked women sexfighting.'

'You know neither of these has anything to do with sex. They are brilliant interpretations of the human psyche.'

'You see what you see. I see what I see. I will take the sexfight painting. Thank you, Stacy.' She gave the older woman a tight hug, pressing her breasts deep into her friend's larger breasts, ensuring that their nipples brushed over each other. She planted a tender kiss on the brunette's neck, while holding the embrace longer than she normally would.

Stacy loved to hug her sexy friend, but she soon realised this was more than just a friendly hug. This confirmed her earlier thoughts that the younger woman might have been flirting with her over the last few days. This slightly bothered her, as she was afraid they might be getting too close to a line she was not comfortable to cross, having sex with her best friend's daughter.

On the other side, the brunette could not help but to feel good about it. Celeste was a very sexy young woman who could bed almost anybody she wanted. This meant that if the redhead had been flirting with her, she must be thinking that she was also a very sexy woman. She thought about having a talk with Celeste, but decided against it as she still saw the flirting as harmless fun. *'If she is indeed flirting with me'*, she rushed to complete her thoughts.

The next morning, after showering, Celeste decided to no longer wear a bra at home. She wanted her older friend to clearly see her nipples poking through her tops, especially when they stood proudly on her breasts. She also wanted the brunette to feel her breasts and nipples better when they hugged each other, which they often did. As it was a pleasant day, she picked a thin blue blouse with a low-cut neckline and which only reached halfway between her breasts and her midriff. This left her flat tummy and ample amounts of her C-cup breasts on display. She completed her outfit with the tiniest red thong in her closet and a very short and very tight black miniskirt and sandals. The skirt highlighted her shapely thighs and tight bum.

The redhead had a good look at her sexy body in the mirror, making sure it was presented in a sexy, but not too slutty way, before she headed for the breakfast nook.

Stacy looked up when her housegueast entered and, for a moment, lost track of what she was busy with. The young woman looked stunning, even sexier than usual. She immediately noticed that the redhead was not wearing a bra, as her stiff nipples were poking little hills into the fabric of her thin top. The older woman's eyes wandered to the flat tummy and then to the shapely thighs before returning to her friend's face, which had a smug smile on it.

Stacy immediately realised that the redhead dressed this way for her benefit. This flattered her. It felt good to know such a beautiful young woman wanted to impress her enough to dress in such a sexy way.

'Morning, Stacy.' Celeste headed over for their morning hug and kiss.

'Morning, honey.' Stacy opened her arms to invite the younger woman in. Their beautiful bodies pressed tightly together, with their breasts in close contact and their nipples brushing over each other with every slight movement.

'You are such a good hugger. I feel so at ease and at the same time excited when you hold me.' Celeste turned her head and planted a soft kiss just under her friend's ear.

'It is always nice to get a hug from you, honey.' Stacy thought they were about to break the hug, but the younger women still held her tightly. Only a thin blouse covered the breasts pressing into hers, so the brunette could clearly feel the C-cup breasts and long, stiff nipples against her own breasts and nipples. This was very enjoyable, and she almost got lost in the feeling.

'There is no better way to start the day than to feel your body against mine.' The younger woman moved slightly to rub their nipples over each other.

'Breakfast will get cold if I do not dish up.' The brunette let go of her young friend and pulled away. She knew the redhead was flirting with her again, and although this was fun, she had to end it before she got drawn into the pleasure too much.

While they were having breakfast, Stacy caught the redhead looking at her with a lustful look. This flattered her. Her tight body was a product of hours of sweat in the gym and she took great care with her hair and make-up. All this effort was clearly not in vain.

After breakfast, the two women cleaned up before brewing a pot of coffee. After pouring two mugs, they went to the lounge to relax for a while. Stacy sat down on her favourite couch and the redhead sat down on a couch facing hers. They were discussing the monthly poker game Stacy played with three of her friends, which the brunette was hosting that night. Celeste leaned forward to rub her calf. This made her breasts pop out of her low-cut blouse even more than before.

This move caught her friend's attention. She enjoyed the view for a few seconds, thinking this display of young, firm breasts was purely accidental. But when the redhead glanced up at her with a naughty smile on her face, while now slowly and sensually gliding her hand over her thigh, she realised the morning's flirting was still continuing.

A few minutes later, the young woman leaned back in the couch, before sliding her bum forward, allowing her mini to ride up, exposing her legs all the way up to her tight bum. From the brunette's position, she could see the redhead's butt cheeks peeking out as well as glimpses of the red thong covering her pussy.

Stacy knew very well that her young friend was intensifying her flirting game. This did not bother her much as she was certain this was all just innocent fun and that she could stop the flirting anytime it went too far. She took a good look, fully appreciating the beauty of a sexy female body. When they got up to go to the shops a few minutes later, the brunette's nipples were rock hard and her panty moist.

Chapter 5 - Poker

While they were picking out snacks and drinks for the poker game, one of the other three women phoned Stacy to excuse herself from the evening's game.

'It seems there will be a spot for you at the table tonight. Wendy cannot make it tonight. Are you in?'

'Yes, I would love to play if your friends won't mind.'

'They would love to take your money.' Both women laughed.

'How much are the stakes?'

'Not that much, don't worry. It is mainly for fun, but we are all competitive women, so there needs to be some money to play for.'

'As you know, I hate losing. I may just be more competitive than any of you.'

'We will see tonight. I think you are underestimating the will to win of women my age.' Stacy almost said *of sexfighters* but caught herself just in time. Like herself, the other three regular players were all sexfighters against all of whom she had at least one erotic contest.

'My generation take what we want with no mercy. Your generation is way too well-mannered to compete with us.'

'That's where you have it wrong. We also take what we want, but with a smile on our faces instead of a snarl.'

Both women enjoyed the verbal sparring. While talking, both thought of how many sexfights they had won against the other's generation. This made each of them confident that her generation was indeed better and more competitive than the other's generation.

While queuing at the tills to pay for their groceries, Celeste gently placed a tuft of hair, which was hanging over her older friend's forehead, back in place. While doing so, she ensured that her fingers gently brushed over the brunette's skin.

'Thank you, darling.' The gentle touch made the brunette shiver slightly with delight. To anybody else watching, this must have seemed like a kind gesture, but after the effort the redhead had put in to flirt with her, Stacy was sure this was more flirting. She found the public flirting very exciting and hoped for more, but it was their turn to pay for their groceries, so there was no further opportunity for flirting.

That evening, Stacy's two friends, Amelia and Hilde, arrived just after eight. Celeste had seen Hilde before, but did not know Amelia. After the brunette had introduced her young houseguest to her two blonde friends, she offered all a drink before they took their seats at the poker table.

Celeste took the seat opposite from Stacy, with Hilde on her right and Amelia on her left. She tried to remember where she had seen the blonde to her right before. It dawned on her that it had been when she had dropped in on her mother one Saturday afternoon. Hilde was there, and both women were wearing gowns and were covered in sweat.

Her mother had told her they had just returned from the gym and were about to take a shower. Although this made little sense at the time, she had not pushed the issue. But now she wondered whether she had interrupted a sexfight between the two milfs.

'Ladies, we are playing Texas Holdem. Maximum bet is five chips and minimum one. Good luck.' Stacy was shuffling the cards while sharing the rules with the other three players. She placed them to her right for Amelia to break before dealing two cards to each player, starting with Hilde.

All four women bet aggressively during the first game to establish dominance over the others, but none of them had a particularly good hand. Amelia won the hand with a pair of Jacks. After this hand of mad betting, they settled down. Betting now reflected their hands, with the occasional bluff thrown in to keep the other players on their toes.

Stacy was on a roll, having won three hands in a row, albeit with smallish pots, when she felt a bare foot brushing against her foot. At first, she thought it was accidental, but when she looked up to see a naughty smile on her young friend's face, she knew she was in for a night of flirting. She could not really make a fuss in front of her other two friends. But the main reason she did not say anything was because she found flirting, while others were sitting around the table with them, very exciting.

During the next hand, their feet did not touch again. The brunette started to think the touch had been accidental. But the look on her young friend's face made her realise she was maybe playing games with her to distract her from the game. This proved to be accurate. When the next game started, the redhead's foot touched her foot again, before slowly sliding up to her calf. Her bare toes gently massaged the muscle before slowly gliding up the older woman's leg until reaching her knee.

The anticipation killed Stacy. She wondered whether the foot would explore her thigh, or whether it would head back down to her foot. She was hot with lust. This was not the first time somebody had played footsy with her and her body was anticipating sex, as most previous footsy games had led to hot and steamy sex. Her nipples were erect and her panty was turning moist. The footsy game distracted her to a point where Amelia had to remind her to pick up her cards.

Stacy considered returning the favour. Her foot was eager to explore the redhead's legs, but she stopped herself, fearing that this might give her houseguest hope that something might happen between them. She enjoyed the attention her leg was receiving, though. This did not bother her, as she was sure she could stop the flirting anytime she needed to. To prove this to herself, she moved her leg away a few times, while leaving it to be explored most of the time.

The game of footsy continued under the table while the game of poker continued on top of it. But the two women involved in the hidden game were getting more and more distracted, finding it difficult to focus on the poker game. This meant that they lost most hands, winning only a few where they got lucky with the cards dealt.

Hilde wondered why the redhead and brunette were so distracted. At the end of a hand, when they had to give their cards back to the next dealer, she dropped one on purpose. When she bent down to pick it up, she saw Celeste's bare foot brushing against Stacy's calf.

Hilde could not stay long enough to establish whether this was an accidental touch or something more fun, without raising suspicion. She had been in two sexfights against Stacy and had lost both. Although she did not plan to face the sexfight queen soon again, she wondered whether Celeste might be a sexfighter or whether she simply liked to fuck other women.

'I love poker. There are so many games going on at the same time.' Hilde smiled at Celeste while saying this.

'Were you bluffing again?' Amelia was not aware of the games underneath the table and thought her friend had been talking about the mind games people play during a poker game.

'I think our young friend to my left has been bluffing for a while.'

'It's poker. Everybody is bluffing.' Celeste blushed slightly as she knew what Hilde was talking about.

Having lost two sexfights against Stacy, Hilde wondered whether the yound women would be an easier opponent to compete with. Not knowing whether Celeste took part in sexfights, she tested the waters.

Moments later, the redhead felt another bare foot touching hers. She knew it was the blonde to her right, so she moved her foot away. Her mission was to flirt with Stacy and not to have a footsy orgy. *Maybe I will teach this old slut a sexfight lesson soon. But I can't be distracted by another lusty bitch now,'* she thought

Hilde removed her foot from the footsy playing field. The young woman was obviously not interested, at least not right then. But Hilde knew the hunt had only just begun. She would definitely test the waters in the future again.

After the poker game ended with Amelia winning all the chips, the four women had a few drinks before the two blondes got up to leave. When Stacy hugged and kissed Amelia, Celeste used the opportunity to get close to Hilde, as she had decided to make the blonde her next sexfight target after pursuing the brunette. She hugged the older woman tightly, ensuring that their breasts pressed together.

While they were in close contact, she whispered into the blonde's ear. 'It is not over. We will test each other next time, bitch.'

Hilde's nipples grew stiff while she pulled the redhead even closer and whispered in her ear. 'I can hardly wait, you slut. Call me when you are ready.'

They broke their hug and bid each other a good night, this time loud enough for the others to hear. After Stacy hugged Hilde and Celeste hugged Amelia, the two blondes went home.

After the blondes had left, the two women returned to the couch to finish their drinks. Stacy looked intently at her young friend for a few seconds while sipping on her wine.

'You've been a naughty girl tonight,' she finally said. She still felt very flattered that the sexy woman flirted with her for most of the poker game, but she wanted to show that there was a line she was not prepared to cross. This was all fun though, and although it turned her on, she was sure she would not cross the line, no matter how much her houseguest's games aroused her.

'I was getting bored. The game was getting boring when you started winning each hand.'

The next afternoon, after taking a brief nap, Stacy went to the kitchen to make a pot of tea. She found Celeste sitting at the kitchen table, shuffling the deck of cards.

'I thought losing so badly would be enough poker for you for a while.' The brunette gave the young woman a cheeky smile.

'Do I have to remind you that you lost all your chips before I did?'

'Only because you distracted me.'

'We were all distracted by your beauty. You do not hear us complaining. Anyway, one of my male friends challenged me to a strip poker game, but I am not sure how to play strip poker.'

'All you need to know is how to play poker and how to take your clothes off.' The brunette had been in many strip poker games and she knew there was much more to strip poker than that. But she also knew that Celeste was looking for an excuse to flirt with her again, so she decided to make her work for it.

'I thought so too, but I have read a few internet pages on the topic and it seems to be more complex than that. The stakes are high for this challenge and I want to be confident when I play against him. Please play with me. I need some practice before I play against him.'

'I won't strip naked with you.'

'We can play only to our underwear. I just need to get a feel for the game.' Celeste gave the older woman her best puppy face expression.

'Okay then, but only a few hands.' The older woman did well to hide her excitement. Strip poker always got her engines running, and playing it with this sexy young woman, who had been flirting with her for a while, made her heart bounce in anticipation. She once again convinced herself this would be harmless fun, which she could control.

'The easiest way to play with only two players is to use five-card draw rules with no betting rounds. The bets are set. For each hand, each of you bet one piece of clothing. After the draw, you open your hands and the loser takes off one piece of clothing. Obviously, you should start with the same number of clothing items.'

'That sounds easy enough. Shall we try it?'

'Okay, but remember, only a few hands.'

After dealing the first hand, Stacy was glad to have two aces in her hand. She swapped her other three cards, but this did not improve her hand. Celeste only swapped one card, but when she showed her hand, it was clear she was going for a flush, but missed it. The pair of aces therefore won the hand for the older woman.

'I won the hand, so you have to remove a piece of clothing.' To the brunette's surprise, the younger woman removed her blouse first. As she had not been wearing a bra around the house for the last few days, this exposed her magnificent breasts. 'Most people would remove their shoes first, but the choice is yours.'

'I just thought if I bare my breasts first, it may distract my friend when we play. Do you think it will work?'

'I am sure it will, but were we not supposed to play to our underwear only?' Stacy could not stop herself from having a quick look at her sexy young friend's full C-cup breasts and long, hard nipples.

'Yes, underwear ... panties.'

'Underwear includes bras.'

'Panties are underwear, bras are upperwear.'

'What?'

'You must move with the times.. The term *upperwear* has been trending for a few years now.' Celeste knew people used this term for something very different than a bra, but she also knew her older friend would not search for its meaning.

'I am sure you are having me on.' Stacy did not really want to bare her breasts during the game, but her competitive side would not allow her to back down now.

The brunette won the next two games, leaving her houseguest without shoes and bare chested. But the redhead made a comeback and won four games in a row. This forced the older woman to strip down to her bra and panties. The next game would determine who would be down to her panties first.

Celeste turned three tens and swapped the other two cards. She was confident in her hand, but hoped for a full house or a four of a kind. Stacy could not be more disappointed in her hand. She had nothing but three non-connecting diamonds. She threw away the other two cards, not having much hope for a decent hand. But she smiled when she received her two new cards. Both were diamonds, giving her a lucky flush.

Celeste threw her cards on the table when she saw the sexy milf's flush. She still had three of a kind and lost the hand.

'I can't believe how lucky you are, drawing two and still getting a flush.'

'You don't have to take off your shorts if you don't want to. The game is over.' The brunette was saying this more for her own benefit, to prove to herself she could stop their flirting whenever she wanted to.

'A competitive woman never refuses to pay up when she loses, at least not competitive women of my generation. Maybe your generation chickens out, but we don't.' Celeste knew this would rile up the older woman.

'Oh, we never back down from a challenge or from settling our debt when we lose.'

'Prove it. I challenge you to five more games.'

'But you will have no more clothes left after taking off your shorts.'

'We play for forfeits. My friend wants us to play for forfeits when we are naked, so I want to practice it with you.'

Stacy had painted herself into a corner. After what she had just said, she could not back down from this challenge, but she also knew what forfeits would lead to. But she convinced herself she could control the situation even if she became hot with lust from the forfeits.

'I accept your challenge, but nothing under the belt and each forfeit lasts thirty seconds only.'

'Deal.' The redhead slowly removed her tight shorts, revealing a tiny red thong which only barely covered her clean-shaven pussy. She enjoyed the way her friend tried not to look at it, but failed miserably. Even with the restrictive forfeit rules, she had high hopes that the forfeits would lead to a sexfight challenge.

Celeste won the next hand, forcing the brunette to remove her skirt to reveal a small black thong, larger than the redhead's tiny thong, but by no mean modest. Both women knew that the next hand would lead to the first forfeit. Both needed to win this hand. Stacy wanted to ensure the forfeits do not get out of hand, while Celeste wanted to arouse the brunette as much as possible.

The redhead was disappointed when she lost the hand, but still hoped her sexy older friend would pick a forfeit which would arouse both of them.

'Give me a sexy dance without touching me.'

This was not what Celeste had hoped for, but she made the dance as sexy as possible. She seductively rolled her hips, while shaking her breasts to make them jiggle and bounce as close as possible to the older woman's face, without making contact. The thirty seconds were up way too soon.

Stacy could not believe how much the dance turned her on. She tried not to show her excitement, although her rock-hard nipples probably gave it away. *Just focus. This is lots of sexy fun, but I cannot allow it to get out of hand,'* she reminded herself.

When the redhead won the next game, she had a huge grin on her face.

'We will hug each other while standing, and hold the hug until the time is up.' Celeste could not wait to feel the naked D-cup breasts pressed into hers.

Stacy hesitated for a moment, but she could not back out of this. Anyway, she had enjoyed their previous hugs. Having their naked breasts in touch had to feel even better. *'I can handle this,'* she reassured herself before moving in for the hug.

Their breasts pancaked each other while the two women pulled each other in tightly. They held this tight hug for a few seconds before letting go slightly. This gave their stiff nipples an opportunity to joust with each other each time either of them moved their upper body slightly.

Celeste almost got lost in the embrace. She had not been this aroused for a long time. *'This is making me so horny. If it does this to me, it must do the same to her, or perhaps even more. My plan is surely working,'* she thought. *'It is just a shame that she wants nothing under the waist. Imagine if we could press our thighs against each other. I am sure my pussy would have reached out for hers. Maybe hers would have reached out for mine as well.'*

Stacy could hold this hug forever. Her yung friend's naked upper body felt so soft and warm, and her breasts so firm. The nipple jousting made her pussy moisten up, while her nipples were as erect as they had ever been. She wondered why she had made the rule of only upper body fun. It would have been so nice if their lower bodies could press together as well.

During their hug, she did not care whether pressing their naked upper bodies together was crossing the line. All she could think about was how much she enjoyed it. She even moved her upper body as well to ensure their nipples were jousting and their breasts were massaging each other.

Their heads were resting on each other's shoulders, with their lips almost touching each other's sensitive necks. Both were tempted to kiss the other's neck, but they refrained from doing so. Instead, Celeste gently caressed the older woman's back. The brunette almost moaned with lust, but she stopped herself, not wanting to show the younger woman just how excited their hug was making her.

They were both disappointed when Stacy's phone alarm warned them that thirty seconds had elapsed. Celeste won the next game again. Her nipples were aching for more attention, so she chose for them to caress each other's nipples.

This time, Stacy did not hesitate. Her nipples also longed for more attention. Any reservations about the level of flirting and sexual contact were far from her mind now. All she could think about was her nipples and her houseguest's fingers caressing them would feel. She did not have long to wonder. Their fingers found each other's stiff nipples and gently rubbed them, while the women looked deep into each other's eyes.

Celeste closed her eyes for a few seconds before opening them again. She found the pleasure from her nipples being gently rubbed overwhelming. Her clit grew hard and her pussy moistened up. *'She must be ready for a sexfight. I am so turned on, I can burst. She surely feels the same.'* The redhead considered challenging her sexy friend right there and then, but she knew if she moved too early, she might ruin her chances of ever having a sexfight against the older woman.

The pure bliss she felt in her nipples made Stacy's clit twitch with excitement. She had rubbed a few nipple orgasms out before, but nobody else had ever come close. This was the first time another woman could get her clit buzzing with nipple work. The redhead had magic fingers, applying just the right amount of pressure on her sensitive nipples. *'This is at an unexpected level. I am much more turned on than I thought I would be. But I am still in control. I can stop this whenever I want to.'* Her reassurance to herself was not as convincing as it had been before.

Both women were left highly aroused when the alarm signalled the end of the thirty seconds.

Stacy fumbled with her cards, her mind not yet focussed after the previous forfeit. When she won the hand, she immediately went for the mild forfeit she had planned. 'Stand behind me and massage my shoulders.' Stacy needed to cool down a bit and more breasts-to-breast action would have turned her way too hot. She therefore specified that the redhead had to massage her from behind.

Celeste did not waste a second. She got behind her older friend, working her thumbs into the tight muscles, making sure she bumped her naked breasts into the brunette's back. She gave the milf's shoulder a soft kiss before massaging it again. When Stacy did not object to the kiss, the younger woman became slightly bolder. She planted another kiss, this time just under the lusty older woman's ear. Once again, Stacy did not object, so she gave her another kiss on the neck. This time the brunette moaned softly while her body shivered with delight. This convinced the redhead that her friend was too hot to stop her from giving her a love bite while massaging her breasts from behind. But the time was up before she could do so.

Stacy could hardly control herself. The pleasure from the kisses to her neck were overwhelming all her senses. If it had carried on any longer, she might not have been able to fight her sexual instincts.

Celeste was still hoping for more. She turned the brunette around before giving her a tight hug, pressing their naked breasts into each other again.

'You did more than I asked', Stacy said as logic and limitations started to return to her mind. The way in which she said this showed that she was not upset, but that she was no longer so horny that she would allow things to escalate.

'My apologies, I was carried away by the moment. Thanks for playing strip poker with me. That was so helpful. It gave me lots of ideas, but I am sure I can learn more from you. I think we should play a few more hands.'

Stacy gently pushed her young friend away from her. 'We have to get dressed. I need to go to the shops.' Although she desperately wanted to feel the sexy young body against hers, and although she would have loved to try out a few more forfeits, she knew her urges were getting too strong and she had to stop right then.

Celeste was very disappointed, but she was careful not to show it. Although she thought she had played her cards right, the failure was just another step towards her ultimate goal, a sexfight with her sexy older friend.

Later, while they were driving to the shops, Stacy had an internal battle with herself. *'That was too close. I must have more control or I must stop these flirting sessions all together. What am I talking about? Of course I have control. I stopped the forfeits, haven't I? It was just good clean fun. Everything was above the waist. There is nothing to worry about.'* Although doubts still tried to enter her brain, she forced them out, not allowing them to take root.

Chapter 6 – The Shopping Spree

As it was an unplanned trip, Stacy had to think of a reason for telling the younger woman they had to get dressed to go to the shops. Lunch was always a good excuse.

'There is a new restaurant which has a variety of healthy choices for lunch. Do you want to try them?'

'I am slightly peckish,' replied the redhead. 'So lunch would be awesome.'

'Good. Maybe we can shop for new tops and then go for lunch. I saw a top on a woman the other day, which I think would look great on me.'

'All tops look great on you.'

'I guess beauty is in the eye of the beholder.'

'If that is true, the beholder has millions of eyes. Just look around and you will see how men and many women stare at you.'

'Maybe they are staring at you, honey.'

'I am sure they are. Who wouldn't? But even my beauty can't stop them from staring at you.' Celeste said this with a cheeky grin on her face.

Although Stacy knew her daughter was probably saying these things to flirt with her, she also knew that the flirting was based on truths. Men, and some women, could not keep their eyes off of her.

When they arrived at the brunette's favourite clothing shop, the women browsed through the blouses and tops. Stacy could not find the top she was looking for, but the women found other tops they liked.

'This would look so sexy on you.' Celeste held a short top in front of the brunette, to form a picture of what it would look like on her, in both their minds.

'That is too short for me, but it would show off your flat tummy beautifully.'

'It will definitely show off your flat tummy as well. I am not leaving here before we both try it on.'

'I may try it on, but I want to see it on you first. If it's too revealing, there will be no reason for me to try it on.'

'You are way too modest. A sexy body like yours should always be on display.'

'Short tops are for young bodies.'

'Short tops are for sexy bodies.'

Stacy smiled at her young friend, knowing she would not let up until she tried on the top. She also felt good about the redhead repeating how sexy her body was. This alone convinced her to try the top on, even if it would be something she would not buy. When they went to the fitting rooms, Celeste followed the older woman into the small booth.

'Are we using the same booth?'

'Yes, we are trying on the same top and we both want to see how it looks on the other.'

'Okay then, but there is not a lot of space in here.'

'We do not need a lot of space. I will try it on first.' The redhead took off her top and then unhooked her bra.'

'Why are you taking your bra off?'

'This is not the kind of top you wear with a bra. I I need to see how it will look the way I will wear it.'

The brunette milf got a good look at her young friend's magnificent breasts and hard nipples. With the small size of the booth, she could not really miss them, even if she wanted to, and she did not want to. Seeing the firm, young breasts jiggle while the redhead was busy putting on the small top, made her own nipples stiffen up. Having the young woman's naked breast so close to her body made her think back to the forfeits during their strip poker game. Stacy longed to feel them against her again. But then they were suddenly covered by the small top, which barely reached the bottom of the beautiful C-cups. Celeste's hard nipples poked through the material, which clung to her breasts. Stacy found this look almost as sexy as the younger woman's naked breasts.

'What do you think?'

'It is very sexy on you. Your breasts look magnificent in it and it shows off you flat tummy. You must buy this.'

'I definitely will. Your turn to try it.' Celeste took the top off and held it while her older friend removed her top. 'Your bra as well. I will not allow you to ruin the look by spoiling this top with a bra.'

The brunette gave an exasperated sigh before unhooking her bra to reveal her slightly sagging D-cups and long, stiff nipples. Although she made a show of how much she did not want to remove her bra, her heart was pounding with excitement when she did. She wanted the younger woman to look at her full breasts. She wanted her to be as aroused as she was.

The woman's naked breasts were only inches apart while the brunette slid the tight top over her head. She struggled to stretch it around her large breasts. When she eventually succeeded, it did not reach all the way, leaving her under-boobs exposed.

'I told you this is not for me.'

'What are you talking about? Under-boob is the new cleavage. It looks fantastic on you.'

'I am not walking around with my breasts hanging out from under my top.'

'All the newest bikinis show some under-boob. You look so sexy in this. You must definitely buy it.'

'I will leave this one to you. They do not have the top I want here. I will look for it again another day.' Stacy tried to remove the top, but it was too tight around her large breasts.

'Here, let me help you.' The redhead grabbed hold of the top, with her hand squeezing in between her busty friend's full breasts and the tight top, before lifting it. With the effort, their bodies squeezed together. When the older woman's large breasts escaped the confines of the tight top, they fell on top of the younger woman's naked breasts. The next movement, to lift the top over the brunette's head, allowed their breasts to mash together, with their stiff nipples also finding each other.

Neither woman moved away after Celeste had completely removed the top. They looked deep into each other's eyes, each seeing the lust in the other. Celeste was extremely horny. She was sure her friend had to be at least as horny as she was. Although she knew they could not have a sexfight in the booth, she considered challenging the brunette to one there and then.

Stacy was also very aroused. Her nipples were searching out their jousting partners, with pulses of pleasure rushing through them every time they rubbed over each other. She was fully into the flirting game, enjoying the sexy, soft body pressing against hers. Knowing that nothing further would happen in the booth, she only had to worry a little about being in control of her lust.

Both women quickly moved apart when somebody suddenly opened the door of the booth next to theirs. This broke the sensual spell they had over each other. While putting their bras and tops back on, their breasts bumped into each other a few more times. Although this was not as enjoyable as pressing their naked breasts together, it still got their engines going each time it happened. When they left the booth, both their panties were soaking wet.

'I will catch up with you. Let me quickly go pay for this. Maybe you can make sure we get a table at the restaurant.' Celeste saw the bikini rack on the way to the tills and wanted to buy tops, which exposed the under-boob, for her and her friend. She knew the older woman would not want one, so she wanted to get rid of her before purchasing the tops.

Stacy was slightly taken aback, wondering why her young friend wanted to get rid of her, but she did not protest. She glanced at the top one more time, considering whether she must buy one as well, maybe just in a larger size. But she was not sure she would ever look as sexy as the younger woman in it, so she almost immediately gave up on the idea.

The restaurant was not too busy when Stacy arrived. A waitress took her to a table at the back, away from the other patrons. This was the last table the waitress had available. If she would place the brunette at any other table, she would lose her to the waitress responsible for that table.

'Thank you. I am waiting for my friend. Will you bring me the wine list while I wait for her?' It was a warm day, and she needed a glass of chilled white wine.

Celeste joined her just as the waitress brought the wine list.

'I am ordering a white wine. Do you want a glass as well?'

'Yes, please. But order a bottle. I don't think one glass will be enough on such a warm day.'

The older woman picked a wine and asked the waitress to bring them a bottle and an ice bucket to keep it chilled. After the waitress left to fetch the wine, the brunette's attention turned to the younger woman's shopping bag.

'So, did you only buy the top?'

'No.'

'What else did you get? Show me.'

'Later, I bought it for a special occasion.'

'Now I am really curious. You have to show me.'

'You will see it soon. I promise.'

The waitress interrupted them when she brought the wine. She poured a glass for each of them before taking their lunch order. The women mostly studied the menu, with only a few brief conversations, until the waitress returned. Stacy ordered fish and a salad, while the redhead ordered a stuffed chicken fillet with a side salad. Both tried to eat healthy food to keep their beautiful bodies in great shape. Their regular workouts at the gym were also essential for their very sexy bodies. During this time of little conversation, Stacy wondered whether she had allowed things to go too far in the fitting room. Although it was just upper body fun, she knew just how horny she had been. But she, once again, concluded that she had full control as nothing happened under the waist.

Shortly after receiving their food, the conversation circled back to the contents of the shopping bag. The brunette was still very curious and did not want to wait to find out what the redhead had bought.

'I will tell you a secret if you show me what you have purchased.'

'I know all your secrets.' Celeste kicked off her right shoe and slowly slid her right foot against the brunette's leg while saying this in a sultry way.

'Oh, you only think you know.' Stacy did not move her leg away. She enjoyed the younger woman's gentle touch on her leg. By now, she expected some flirting, but it still excited her when it came.

'You will still have to wait to see what I bought.' The redhead slid her foot all the way up to the older woman's thigh and then down over her calf muscle again.

'You with your footsy game. I did not know you were such a big fan.' The brunette did not sound annoyed while saying this. In fact, she kicked off her right shoe and also ran her right foot up the younger woman's left leg. *I should take control away from her. Two can play this flirting game. It is time for me to take the flirting initiative,* she thought to herself.

'We like playing footsy. It's harmless, sensual and fun for both of us.' Although the touch to her leg aroused her, the redhead was not about to hand the initiative over that easily. Her right foot continued exploring her friend's leg while she refilled the older woman's glass with more wine.

While sipping on her second glass of wine, Stacy steered the conversation in a different direction for a while, but the footsy game continued under the table. Both women glanced over at the waitress when she came to check on them, but Stacy kept her eyes on the beautiful young woman while she walked away. Celeste saw this and used the opportunity to change the subject back to a more sexual topic.

'Have you ever made love with another woman?' She expected the older woman to steer the conversation away from this subject, but the brunette had drunk just enough wine to be comfortable discussing this with her young friend.

'Making love with them? Only a few times. Most of the time I prefer to fuck their brains out! As you probably know, there is a difference. What about you, honey?'

'Let's just say we have something in common.' Celeste was smiling while saying this. She intensified her leg rubbing, while looking deep into the brunette's eyes.

'You horny bitch!' Stacy was tipsy and said this slightly louder than she wanted to, but still in a teasing way. She also intensified her leg rubbing while returning her young friend's gaze.

'We are both two horny bitches.'

'True', said the brunette while laughing loudly.'

Celeste could see in the older woman's eyes how aroused she was. Her own pussy with moist with lust, so she took her flirting to the next level. She took the older woman's hand in her own, while maintaining eye contact. While looking deep into her eyes, she slowly turned her hand until her index and middle fingers slid between the brunette's index and middle fingers. As soon as they were properly in a scissoring position, she slowly moved her hand to mimic two women tribbing. Both women knew that this was one way sexfighters challenged each other.

'Do you know what two horny bitches do when they meet? They determine who the hornier and the better bitch between them is.' Celeste whispered this, while still looking into the brunette's eyes. She advanced her fingers until the soft flesh at the base of both sets of fingers pressed together.

Stacy was silent for a bit, while organising her thoughts. Her panty was soaking wet from pure lust. She had been in this scenario many times. Almost all of them led to an intense sexfight, of which she had won most. While thinking, she also moved her hand to trib back with her fingers. This was purely out of habit. When a woman challenged her, she always responded this way to accept the challenge. She still wanted to convince herself this was just a part of the flirty game her young friend was playing with her. However, the pure lust in the redhead's eyes and the intense foot rubbing told her otherwise. They were dangerously close to a line she was not prepared to cross. The brunette milf pulled her hand away to break the tribbing hold, before taking the younger woman's hand in hers.

'This may be right, but I will not be that way with you, honey. Not with you.' She let go of the redhead's hand. 'I had a lot to drink. It is time to go home. I need to go sleep this off.'

When they arrived home, both women tried to ignore what had happened earlier. Stacy was still horny, but she forced any sexy thoughts from her mind. Celeste was also still hot with lust. She replayed the earlier flirting in her mind and could almost feel their breasts press into each other again, and their feet exploring each other's legs. Although the older woman had been firm about not taking things further, she was sure that some more flirting would bring the brunette around.

After having a cup of tea together, Stacy got up to go for a nap. As she did, the redhead also got up and gave her a hug. She made sure their breasts squeezed into each other before going in for a kiss. The hug and their breasts meeting again made the brunette's panty moist with lust. But she got control over her lust when the younger woman tried to kiss her. She gently pushed her away.

'We should not do this. I love it when you are flirting with me. I love it when our breasts touch and when our bodies are in close contact. You make me hot when you flirt with me and I also like flirting with you. But your mother is my best friend. There is a line I will not cross with you.' While her mouth uttered these words, her body was preparing for a revolution. It was hot with lust and ready to beat the younger woman in a sexfight. Stacy's mind was also in turmoil. Although she did not want to cross the line with her best friend's daughter, she also really wanted to beat the young redhead in a competitive sexfight.

This disappointed the younger woman. She had been confident that she could lure the brunette into a sexfight, but now she had been rejected for the second time on the same day. However, instead of giving up, this made the sexy redhead even more determined to flirt with her older friend until she was ready to face her in a sexual contest.

The next morning, Celeste woke up, ready to flirt the pants off of the brunette. The older woman had confessed that she enjoyed their flirting and that it made her hot. It was time to take the flirting to the next level. It was time to make the sexy milf so hot, she would not be able to say no to a sexfight challenge.

The young woman prepared for a day of heavy flirting by putting on her sluttiest blouse, without a bra, her shortest skirt and her tiniest thong. This outfit revealed lots of cleavage, and her bum cheeks flashed with every step she took. She knew this would draw her older friend's attention, but she planned to play it cool, to arouse the milf for a while before making any contact with her.

When Stacy woke up, she needed a coffee. She went down to the kitchen, dressed only in a thin silk nighty, which hung to the middle of her thighs. Her nipples reacted immediately when she saw the redhead parading around in the kitchen in her flimsy outfit. The thin material of her nighty had no chance of hiding her excitement. Although she did not want to give the younger woman the wrong impression, her mind had no say, her body overruled it. It needed to feel the redhead's sexy body against it.

The brunette gave the younger woman a friendly smile. 'Morning, honey' She gave the redhead a tight hug, ensuring that their breast pressed tightly together, while their thighs were also rubbing against each other. Their hard nipples soon found each other and jousted lustily, while they could feel each other's warm breaths against their necks.

Celeste did not plan on physical contact this early in the day. She wanted to build up the sexual energy between them to a point where the older woma could not withstand her advances anymore. But her plan had just been thrown out of the window. The brunette had initiated the flirting, forcing her to rethink her plans. But the tight hug aroused her too much to redraw her plans just yet. Her pussy was already moist and her nipples were trying to push holes through her blouse.

Stacy did not plan the hug. This was something her body did on its own. But she did not regret her body's decision. She thoroughly enjoyed the feeling of the sexy young body pressed into hers. Her naked pussy was so wet under her nighty that she feared it may start dripping on the floor. Each time their silky thighs brushed over each other, her hungry pussy reached out to touch the pussy only inches away from it.

The hug lasted way longer than any of their previous hugs. Celeste only broke it when the water reaching boiling point made the kettle whistle.

'Sit down. I will make you a nice cup of coffee,' said Celeste.

'Thanks, darling. I would do anything for a coffee.'

'Don't make promises you can't keep.'

'Anything within reason, then. Maybe the hug was payment enough. I can see how much you've enjoyed it.' The brunette said this with a smile, casting her eyes over the younger woman's stiff nipples poking little hills into her blouse.

'Nah, that can't be payment. You've enjoyed it at least as much as I did.' The redhead looked at the stiff nipples, clearly visible through the thin silk. She was not nearly as discreet as her older friend. Hers was a proper stare, rather than a glance.

'What do you suggest as payment, then?' Negotiating for some kind of sexy payment, turned the brunette extremely hot. She expected at least a topless hug, which she was eager to do again. In her mind, anything above the waist was fair game, except for a sensual kiss. That was too intimate.

'I bought something, which you must promise to wear at the swimming pool this afternoon.'

This disappointed Stacy slightly, but she did not show it. Then she got concerned. 'What do you want me to wear?'

'Don't look so frightened. It is just something slightly sexier than what you would normally wear. But I promise you, it will look very good on you.' After handing her friend's coffee to her, she smiled at her. 'You look so tense. Sit down so that I can rub your shoulders while you are having your coffee.'

When the brunette sat down, Celeste slid the nighty's straps from her shoulders before gently rubbing and massaging the tight muscles.

Stacy sighed deeply while her young friend worked at the knots in her shoulders. Although most of the touches massaged the shoulders, some touches, especially to her neck, were very tender and loving, causing pulses of pleasure to rush to her brain. She allowed the straps of her nighty to slip down her arms. This allowed the garment to expose her breast further and further, the more she leant forward. Only her stiff nipples stopped it from falling all the way to her waist.

Celeste enjoyed the way the brunette's large breasts jiggled each time she put some effort in to loosen the muscles. This captivated her attention. She could not take her eyes off of the brunette's breasts. The way they moved and jiggled was almost magical. The redhead's nipples were burning for attention, so she pressed her breasts onto her friend's back, moving her upper body slightly to rub her nipples against it.

Feeling the redhead's breasts push into her back, excited the brunette. She sighed even deeper than before. These sighs were partly from her muscles being massaged, but mostly from lust.

Celeste slowly moved her hands until they were massaging the sides of the older woman's breasts while tenderly kissing her neck.

'You are pushing it, honey. We have talked about boundaries.' Stacy's voice was husky with lust, and she did not sound very convincing.

'I know you like it. Besides, this is not an erotic kiss and all the kissing and touching is above the waist. I am not crossing your precious line.' Celeste whispered this in a sultry voice between kisses to her friend's neck. As the milf did not get upset and also did not move her neck away, or tried to remove the younger woman's hands from her breasts, Celeste continued kissing and massaging.

The brunette was getting very aroused, but then her phone rang. She glanced at it and gave a sigh, this time out of frustration.

'It is the office, honey. I have to take this.' As Stacy was on leave, she knew the office would only phone her for urgent matters. She, therefore had to take the call.

'We will cross these fucking lines. You are almost ready, it's coming soon.' Celeste muttered this to herself, knowing that the older woman, who had walked to another room to take the call, would not hear this promise she made to herself. Her sexy older friend had told her that she might have to work during her leave, but the redhead could not believe how bad the timing of this call had been.

After the call, Stacy gave the sexy redhead a sweet smile. 'Thank you. That was one of the most pleasurable massages I've ever had. I need to log on for an urgent client meeting. We will continue this later.'

Chapter 7 – Slutty When Wet

After two hours of meeting with the client and then with her team, Stacy eventually joined her houseguest on the couch. 'I am sorry. That took a lot longer than I thought it would. Unfortunately, I will have to work again later. My team will bring me an opinion I have to review and sign off. But it will be a few hours before I have to work again. Do you want to do something before then?'

'It is fine. I know you have work responsibilities. Maybe we can go for a swim.' Celeste was aware of the older woman's agreement with her office, but she was still slightly disappointed that the brunette had to work.

'That is a fantastic idea. It is such a lovely day. Some tanning and swimming are just what the doctor ordered.'

'Good, it is time for you to pay for that coffee. I want you to wear a bikini top I have picked out for you.'

'Just how small is this bikini top?'

'It is a D-cup. Don't worry, I will wear the same design. It is sexy, and will look good on both of us.'

'Oh well, give it to me, then.'

'It is on your bed. I already have mine on under my top, so I will take glasses and a bottle of wine to the pool. Don't make me wait too long.' The redhead said this in a flirty way, preparing the milf for some heavy flirting at the pool.

Stacy found the black bikini top on her bed. It was an under-boob bikini, with the inner triangle only covering about half of the outer triangle of each cup. She had seen these before, but never thought of buying one. Showing cleavage was one thing. Showing the under parts of her breasts somehow felt like being topless.

'I've been topless with Celeste before, and nobody else would see us. I guess putting this on will not be the end of the world. It will be great to see her in one of these as well.'

The milf shook her head before stripping naked to put a black string bikini bottom on with the under-boob bikini top. Looking at herself in the mirror, she understood why these were so popular. She turned her body to look at herself from different angles, delighted at how sexy she looked. *'I rock this. But I still will not wear it in public,'* she thought.

Celeste eagerly looked up when her friend entered the swimming pool courtyard. The brunette shimmied her large breasts at the younger woman.

'You've done well. This actually looks good on me.'

'It looks amazing. You are so sexy in that.'

'Thank you. You also look very sexy in yours.'

'Shall we go to the mall in these later to give a few guys heart attacks?'

'We will give a few women heart attacks as well. I prefer to be this sexy in private. My under-boobs are not meant to be viewed by strangers.'

The redhead handed her friend a glass of wine before lifting her own glass. 'Here's to being sexy in private.'

Stacy clinked her glass against that of the younger woman. 'To being sexy in private.'

The two women got into the pool while sipping on their wine. They enjoyed the cool water for a while before Celeste's competitive side kicked in.

'Shall we have a race like we used to do when I was younger?'

'You do understand that I allowed you to win back then. You are all grown up now, so I will beat you with a smile on my face.'

'Even back then, I was slowing down not to humiliate you. Today, I will not have any mercy.'

'What are we racing for?'

'The loser washes the winner's back when we shower afterwards.'

'Are we showering together?'

'We will have to for the back washing.'

Stacy considered pointing out that they could easily pick something else to race for, but could already imagine how good it would feel when her sexy young friend would wash her back.

'Deal. We swim four lengths, starting inside the pool. The one who touches this wall first, after the four lengths, wins.'

'Shall we hug on it?'

'Do you mean shake..? Okay, that actually sounds about right. Let's hug on it.'

The two women eagerly pressed their scantily clad bodies together. Their naked under-boobs felt so good against each other that both wanted to hold the hug. But both were also eager to compete against the other. They broke the hug rather quickly for their recent history, but still held it longer than a friendly hug would last.

'Are you ready?'

'Just wait a moment.' The redhead removed her bikini top.

'And now?'

'The top may increase resistance. I want to be as streamlined as possible.'

Stacy was sure the top would make no difference in their swimming speed, but she also did not want to take any chances. Her competitive nature trumped her modesty. But her choice to remove her top, was mainly because it excited her to compete with the redhead while being topless.

After the women entered the water, Celeste counted backwards from three before they started swimming. They were neck and neck at the first turn, with the brunette turning just slightly in front. She maintained her slight lead with the second turn, but they were dead-even at the third turn. When they reached the wall for the end of the race, both were convinced they had touched first.

'I told you I would beat you.' Celeste had a huge smile on her face.

'You are joking, right? I clearly beat you.'

The smiles on both ladies' faces turned to a bemused look. Neither could believe the other was trying to claim the victory. They turned to each other, while still standing in the shallow end of the swimming pool. Their naked, wet breasts pressed into each other as neither would take a step backwards. With their faces only inches apart, the women glared at each other, both thinking the other was cheating.

'Come-on, admit that I've beaten you.' Stacy looked straight into the redhead's eyes.

'You may think you've won, but I know I have touched the wall first.' Celeste returned her friend's gaze.

The women's naked breasts bumped into each other with every gesture made during their argument. Both were certain they were right, but both also knew the other believed the same and would therefore not back down. They loved each other too much to let the outcome of their race get out of hand.

'I am prepared to wash your back if you also wash mine.' Stacy came up with a solution, which required neither of them to back down.

'I agree to that.' Celeste realised this was the best solution for their disagreement. She and her older friend had their fair share of arguments, but they loved each other too much to hold a grudge or to allow an argument to carry on for too long. The redhead also did not want to ruin their flirty mood by arguing too aggressively.

With their bodies already pressed together, the women hugged each other tightly to make peace and to seal the deal they had just made. Both ensured that their breasts, tummies and thighs were in close contact with each other. Their stiff nipples sought each other out and eagerly jousted in a sensual duel. Both women thrusted their hips forward to allow their lower bodies to touch each other lightly. For a moment, their pussies touched through their bikini bottoms. But Stacy quickly returned to reality, realising she was breaking her own rule of keeping their flirting above their waists. She gave her houseguest a kiss on the cheek before breaking their embrace.

Both women were very hot with lust. Their pussies, having touched briefly, were ready for a sexual contest with each other. Their breasts were longing for the soft embrace of the other woman's breasts and their stiff nipples needed to duel with their stiff counterparts.

As Stacy moved away from her friend, it took all of her focus not to grab hold of the redhead again. Her whole being wanted to have a sexfight with the sexy young woman. It was only her determination not to cross the Rubicon which kept her moving backwards.

Celeste could not believe that her very attractive older friend was mentally strong enough to break away from her. She was on the edge of no return, and she could see the same level of lust in the brunette's eyes. She had to force herself not to follow the milf. Although she was almost sure the brunette could not withstand more physical contact, she decided to wait for a time where she was totally sure her friend was ready for a sexfight.

After getting out of the pool and drying off, the two women lay down on the pool chairs to tan their sexy bodies. As they were topless already, they could get a nice, even suntan on their upper bodies.

'Must I help you apply some suntan lotion to your body?' Celeste tried to sound as innocent as possible, although she knew that her friend would surely see this for what it was, more flirting.

'Please help me with my neck, shoulders and back.' The brunette was about to turn her bikini bottom into a thong to ensure her bum would also get an even suntan. But she decided to leave it covering her bum until after the younger woman had applied the suntan lotion. Exposing her tight bum might just be seen as an invitation to apply lotion to it as well.

The redhead gently applied lotion to her older friend's neck before moving to her shoulders and then her back. The gentle touch turned the milf hot again. The redhead's fingers lit up the sensory receptors in Stacy's skin, sending sensations of pleasure to her brain. This state of bliss she was in made her more receptive to contact with her bum.

After finishing her friend's back, Celeste moved the bikini bottom over the brunette's bum cheeks and wedged it between them, turning it into a thong. Without hesitation, she applied lotion to the milf's tight bum, before moving on to her thighs.

Stacy enjoyed the soft touch to her bum too much to object. When wearing a bikini bottom, she always turned it into a thong when tanning. She could hardly get upset with the redhead for helping her with the process and then ensuring that her bum would not get burnt by the sun. It slightly disappointed her when her sexy young friend moved away from her bum, but the joy continued when lotion was applied to her legs, especially when the younger woman rubbed it onto her inner-thighs. The brunette was so hot with lust, she could explode.

'Shall I do your front as well?' Celeste still tried to sound all sweet and innocent.

'No, I will do my front. I just needed help with the areas I cannot reach.' Stacy had to force herself to say this. Her whole body was crying out for the sexy young woman to rub lotion all over her breasts and all the way down to her pussy. But she could not take any chances, knowing how close she had been earlier to cross the line with her best friend's daughter.

The redhead waited until her friend had covered the front of her body with lotion before continuing, all sweet and innocent. 'Will you please help me with the lotion?'

'Sure, honey.' Stacy also started with the neck and worked her way down. She loved the way her sexy young friend's smooth skin felt and spent more time on her back than was necessary. Although she had planned to only apply suntan lotion to the back of the redhead's upper body, the younger woman's tight little bum looked so good in her tiny thong, she could not resist. *It is just a bum. It will only take a moment to apply the lotion. I can handle touching her bum for a moment.* But her hands stayed on the sexy bum way longer than planned. She just could not get enough of the soft, yet firm orbs.

The brunette was also very aroused when her hands eventually moved to the younger woman's athletic legs. The silky-smooth skin and the sexy curves of the redhead's legs aroused her even more. When done, she was tempted to slap the young bum, but she just managed to stop herself from doing so. Her arousal levels were dangerously high again. Knowing how difficult it had been to move away from the redhead earlier, she had to stop herself before it would be too difficult to withstand the younger woman's charms.

Celeste fully enjoyed her older friend's hands on her body. She loved how lusty this made her. When the brunette applied lotion to her bum, she had to stop herself from moaning loudly. This also gave her hope that the brunette was at last ready to move to the next level.

'That was so sensual. Do you want to do my front as well?' Celeste turned around, pressing out her breasts invitingly.

'I think you better do that yourself.'

'Did you not enjoy oiling me up?'

'I did, but maybe too much.'

'It is all just an innocent bit of fun.'

'You act all innocent, but I think you are a naughty girl.'

'Maybe I am slightly spicy.'

'I am sure you are, but I have to draw the line somewhere, and I think it better be here.'

From the tone of her friend's voice, Celeste was sure the brunette just needed some more time and some skillful flirting to cross the line. She gave her sexy older friend a sweet smile while sensually applying suntan lotion to her full breasts, pulling gently on her own nipples while doing so. The show moved to her flat tummy, with her hands flirting with her own pussy as they moved to her inner thighs before moving down her legs.

Stacy could hardly contain her lust while watching the sexy show. She was openly staring, and although she knew the redhead was enjoying this, she could not get herself to avert her eyes.

Celeste had a confident smile on her face when they lay down next to each other to tan. She had the brunette just where she wanted her and was sure she would be successful with her next flirting effort. She could not wait for them to shower together later.

After tanning for a while, Stacy got up. 'I need to shower and dress before my colleague brings the opinion for me to review. You are welcome to tan some more.' The brunette said this to pretend their planned back washing session was not important to her, but she truly hoped the younger woman would join her in the shower. Her nipples stiffened up while she was thinking about how the redhead's wet body would feel against hers.

'I am also done. You owe me a backwash. Don't think you will get out of that.' Celeste was also very lusty and would never allow the opportunity for further flirting to pass her by.

'Oh, yes. You owe me a backwash as well.'

Both women tried to act cool, but neither was fooling the other. Their lust made their voices husky and their eyes hungry. Neither woman bothered to put her bikini top back on. This allowed their magnificent breasts to swing freely while they made their way to the house. Both glanced over at the other's jiggling orbs, enjoying the sexy show.

They entered the house and rushed to the bathroom, eager to get wet with each other. While Stacy opened the taps to get the water temperature just right, Celeste removed her thong. She found it difficult to wait any longer and considered pulling the brunette's bikini bottom down as well. But she restrained her lust and waited for the milf to remove her own bikini bottom.

Both women were clean shaven, always keeping their sexfight weapons ready for combat. Although they tried to be discreet, the two lusty women openly stared at each other's juicy pussies before entering the shower. This time, when their sexy naked bodies pressed into each other, neither woman pulled away.

'I will wash your back first.' Celeste's voice was thick with lust. She took the soap and waited until the brunette's back was nice and wet before she used a loofah to lather up the milf's back. She made sure that her hips pressed up against her naked friend's tight bum, while her breasts regularly bumped into her back.

Stacy was breathing heavily, while her body shivered in delight. Feeling her sexy younger friend's naked body pressed up against hers drove her wild with lust. She moaned softly every time she felt the redhead's soft breasts and hard nipples against her skin. Her resistance was quickly crumbling. *'Maybe I should teach this young bitch a sexfighting lesson. The youthful arrogance is strong with her. With my experience I can show her she has much to learn still.'* Stacy's sexy thoughts made her even more aroused. The doubts which had normally entered her mind during and after their flirting were nowhere to be found. She was almost ready to cross the line.

'My turn. You have to wash my back now.' Celeste wanted to feel her friend's hands on her body. She hoped to feel her breasts against her back as well. The young woman was ready to explode from lust, but she was not sure whether the brunette was at the right level to have a sexfight against her. She did not want to make her move too soon again.

Stacy did not bother with the loofah. She lathered her hands with soap before gently rubbing her young friend's sexy back with it. Her pussy was screaming for attention, so she pressed her hips tightly against the redhead's tight bum to place their pussies as close to each other as she could. Her large breasts gently slapped against the younger woman's back while she deliberately moved her upper body more than needed to wash the shapely back.

Feeling her the older woman's crotch pushed up against her bum, Celeste leaned forward with her hands spread against the wall and pushing her pussy as far backwards as she could. 'If you weren't my mom's best friend, I would do unspeakable things to you.'

'If you weren't my best friend's daughter, I would teach you a sexfighting lesson,' replied Stacy in a voice thick with lust.

These words were not entirely true. Both women were more than ready to cross the line. Both understood exactly what the other was actually saying. It was time to take their flirting to the next level. It was time to test each other's sexual skills in a sexfight.

When Stacy's hands wandered to find the redhead's firm C-cups, the younger woman got back upright and turned around.

The two women pushed their wet bodies tightly together. Their pussies reached out for each other, but just could not reach. Their flat tummies and large breasts squeezed into each other, while their stiff nipples sought each other out for a sensual joust. The two lusty women looked deep into each other's eyes before their lips met for a kiss. It was gentle at first, but soon got more urgent. Just when they were about to explore each other's mouths with their hungry tongues, the doorbell rang.

Stacy broke their kiss, but Celeste immediately moved in to lock their lips again. The kiss convinced the brunette to ignore the bell, but then her phone rang, before the bell rang again. This brought her back to reality. It must be the office. She broke their kiss again, this time gently pushing the younger woman away from her.

'It is the office. I have to go.'

'Ignore them.'

'I wish I could.' The brunette quickly got out of the shower and wrapped a towel around her before answering the door.

'Hi Julie. Sorry about the towel. I just had a swim.'

The thirty-year-old blonde manager gave her a sweet smile. 'Hi Stacy. I am so sorry we have to bother you with this.'

'No problem. Come in and sit down. Give me a few minutes to get dressed. I will make us something to drink after I am more decent.'

'Let me make the coffee. Do you want yours the same as at the office?'

'Yes, that is sweet of you. My friend is in the shower. Just pop your head in and ask her what she wants as well.'

While Stacy went to her room to get dressed, Julie followed the sound of splashing water to find the bathroom where Celeste was showering. She slowly opened the door and peeked her head through. She was about to ask what the redhead wanted to drink, but then she realised that the young woman was feverishly playing with herself. Her back was turned to the door, so she was not aware of the blonde. This gave Julie a chance to watch, while her nipples grew stiff and her pussy moist. Watching the sexy, young woman rub herself off, aroused her more than she thought it would. After watching for a while, she carefully closed the door and headed for the kitchen, deciding to make something for the redhead later.

When Stacy returned to the lounge, she sipped on her coffee while the blonde briefed her on the facts and the research and interpretation used to draft the opinion.

'That sounds good, but I think we should explore the tax implications of the connected parties a bit more. Let me read through the draft opinion first, then we can discuss it further.'

Moments later, Celeste came into the lounge, covered only in a towel. When Stacey introduced the two younger women to each other, she noticed that Julie blushed before averting her eyes. It took the brunette a few seconds to put two and two together. She had left her young friend in the shower in a highly aroused state. A few minutes later, she had sent Julie into the bathroom. Clearly her colleague had walked in on the redhead pleasuring herself.

'So Julie, I assume Celeste did not want coffee.'

'Urm... I did not know which bathroom, so I did not ask.'

'It was the one I showed you.'

'I did not want to disturb her while...'

'Stacy!' Celeste realised what must have happened. 'Stop torturing Julie. Julie I am sorry. I did not know you came into the bathroom.'

'It is alright. We all do it. I should have knocked.'

There was an awkward silence before Stacy changed the subject. 'Well, as much as I enjoy watching your discomfort, we have work to do.'

The work they still needed to do to ensure the opinion covered all potential risks, took longer than Stacy had hoped for. By the time Julie left with all the required changes made to the document, she needed a nap. She also needed to figure out what had happened in the shower earlier.

Now that the black-haired milf was no longer very horny, her mind was in conflict with itself. If it was not for Julie arriving at a crucial time, she would probably have had a sexfight with her young friend. She wanted to be more upset with herself for allowing things to go so far, but somehow she felt at peace with her actions. Having a sexfight with the younger woman seemed so right. *How could I justify doing this? How can I justify not doing it? Maybe I should sleep on it and think about it again when I am well rested.*

When the brunette knocked on her houseguest's bedroom door to wish her a good night's sleep, the redhead did not answer, although Stacy could hear movement inside. She thought about going to bed without saying goodnight, but decided against it. After knocking again, she slowly pushed the door open. The sight inside made her nipples jump to attention. The redhead had her earphones in, dancing to music. She had her back to the door and was dressed only in a tiny blue thong with a matching bra.

Stacy was mesmerized by the way the sexy young body moved to the rhythm of the music. She considered leaving, or at least making the young woman aware that she was there. But her body refused to move and her tongue refused to form any words. She stood in the door, allowing the sexy show to arouse her.

Celeste was almost in a trance while listening to her favorite tunes. Her body was moving on its own, doing what came naturally to it. When she glanced up at her mirror, she saw her older friend watching her. This made her feel sexy. She carried on as if she did not know the brunette was watching her, but slowly built up the sexiness of her dance. Her hips were swaying slightly more, making her bum cheeks jiggled slightly more.

Stacy no longer cared about how to explain her presence should the redhead turn around. All she cared about was not to do anything which would disturb the show. Her nipples were now rock hard and her pussy moist. The sexy show turned her on, but she was still in control, knowing that she still had to decide how far she was prepared to go with her sexy young friend.

Celeste did not have to look in the mirror again. She could feel the brunette's eyes following her every move.

'Are you enjoying the show? Maybe I should start charging people to watch me enjoy myself.' The tone in her voice was relaxed, and in no way upset. It was clear she was enjoying the attention. The redhead still had her back turned on her friend and continued dancing.

'I did not want to disturb you, honey. You look like you are truly enjoying yourself.'

'I am, but I think you are truly enjoying yourself as well.'

'I am. You are putting on one hell of a show. I have a stripper ... friend.' The brunette did not want to use the term 'sexfight opponent' just yet. 'She could learn a few moves from you.'

'Like this?' The sexy young woman unhooked her bra while still facing away from her older friend. When she turned around, her hands covered her breasts, gently massaging them. She walked towards the brunette seductively, keeping eye contact. When she was only a few feet away, she stopped before removing one hand and then the other.

Stacy tried to keep eye contact with the sexy young woman, but the gravitational pull of the perfectly shaped C-cups with their stiff, long nipples was too strong. Her gaze soon went down to the perfect breasts.

This brought a satisfied smile to the redhead's face. She had the brunette where she wanted her, lusting after her sexy young body. It was time to implement the master plan she had thought out while waiting for her friend to finish working.

After giving the redhead's body one more good look, the older woman bid her a good night before going to her room.

The brunette was in deep thought, preparing herself to get some sleep, when there was a knock on the door. Moments later, Celeste entered, wearing only her thong.

'I'm going to fuck Julie's brains out,' she announced, trying to look cool. 'You know that, don't you?'

This shocking announcement pulled the brunette's mind back to reality. Her sex life and work life never mixed. They were in two different galaxies, light years away from each other, never to meet. Sure, she enjoyed the sight of some of her colleagues, but she would never cross the line with anybody from the office.

She also could not allow her friend to seduce a colleague, especially not somebody like Julie, who she worked closely with on many projects.

'You stay away from her. I do not want a mess at the office when the two of you break up.'

'I don't want to date her. I just want to fuck her.'

'Even worse. I will not allow this.' Stacy walked right up to her topless friend, getting right in her face. Her breasts pushed into the naked C-cups, with their stiff nipples now jousting in anger.

'You do not have a choice,' Celeste protested. She ensured their breasts kept grinding together, knowing her older friend enjoyed this as much as she did. She wanted every advantage she could use to get the brunette to go along with her plan. 'I am an adult, so is she. She is clearly lusting after me. It is my duty to help out a sweet girl like her.'

'This is not an option. My colleagues are off limits.'

'All of them, or just Julie? I saw the way you looked at her earlier. Maybe you want to fuck her first.' The look on her friend's face told Celeste she was spot on. 'I will wrestle you for her. If you beat me in a wrestling match, I will obey your rules.'

'I am much stronger than you.'

'Maybe, but I have more wrestling skills and I am fitter and faster than you. Are you scared to wrestle me?'

Her young friend's arrogance pushed Stacy over the edge. She could not back out of this wrestling challenge, even if she wanted to. 'All right then,' she said. 'We will wrestle. It is about time I put you in your place.'

'I am ready', her sexy, topless friend replied. 'Shall we go to the gym?' Stacy's gym room in her large house had an exercise mat, which was more than big enough for them to have a wrestling match on.

'We will wrestle in my gym, but not tonight. I am tired and need to go to bed. We will settle this first thing tomorrow morning.' Stacy's excuse that she was tired was true, but she also needed some time away from her friend to cool down and to decide on how far she was prepared to go with her.

'A duel at dawn, then. It can hardly get more exciting than that.' The redhead leaned in and gave her older friend a tight hug, pressing their breasts even deeper into each other. 'You better have a good rest. You will need all your strength tomorrow.'

'I will be ready. You do not know what your mouth got you into this time.' Stacy gave her young friend a loving kiss on the forehead to show there was no animosity, but her words made it clear this would be a competitive wrestling match.

Stacy was ready to leave her friend's bedroom when a thought stopped her. 'I was thinking. If I win tomorrow, I will get to seduce Julie. What do you get if you win? Is there something I can do for you should you be victorious?' The redhead gave her older friend a seductive smile.

'The wrestling match is about Julie. I accepted your challenge, but do not get the wrong idea, honey. As I told you, I like our flirting. It flatters me. It's hot and I need some carefree and hot moments. Yes, I love to sexfight with other women, especially women younger than me, to tame them.But I have no intension to cross any red lines with my best friend's daughter! We will have match to stop you from fucking Julie or from even just hitting on her. But it will strictly be wrestling, nothing more.'

'You and your fucking lines. Anyway, see you tomorrow.' The redhead was slightly fed up. She had been so sure her plan was coming together, but now her older friend was giving her a cold shoulder again. She shut the door, slightly harder than necessary, leaving Stacy alone in her bedroom.

However, after getting back to her room and calming down, Celeste was still sure her friend would not be able to resist her charms once their sexy bodies would struggle against each other in close combat. She was sure her plan would work and that she and the brunette would also have a sexfight against each other the next day.

Stacy knew how horny a wrestling match against another sexy woman could make her. She had to be clear on her intentions before their wrestling match. If she did not want the wrestling match to turn into a sexfight, she would have to focus on winning and push any desires from her mind.

Chapter 8 – The Duel at Dawn

When Stacy woke up the next morning, she was clear about how far she was prepared to go with her young friend. She brushed her teeth and had a long, hot shower before deciding on her outfit for the wrestling match. For self-defense classes, she usually used a wrestling singlet or gym shorts and a crop top. She also had a few more slutty outfits for wrestling matches against some of her sexfight opponents. Although they mainly had sexfights against each other, they sometimes chose just to have a competitive wrestling match. But she knew her slutty young friend would wear only a tiny thong for their match, and did not want to lose the mental contest about who dared to wear the least. After browsing through her swimwear, she picked a tiny white thong which just barely covered her pussy.

After throwing a gown over her mostly naked body, she headed for the gym, wondering whether Celeste was still sleeping, or whether she was also ready for their showdown. When she opened the gym door, the redhead was already sitting on her knees on the mat, wearing a micro thong, with her body covered in baby oil.

'I was wondering whether you would chicken out.' The younger woman tossed a bottle of baby oil to her opponent.

'Oil wrestling? We did not agree to this.' Stacy knew that the oil would neutralize her strength advantage, as it would make it difficult to apply any holds on the younger woman.

'You don't have to apply oil to your body, but I already did, so the choice is yours.'

'I will still beat you. A slippery body will not stop me from dominating you.' The brunette took off her gown and started oiling up her beautiful body.

Celeste quietly watched how her older friend's sexy body transformed into an even more sexy version of itself, as the oil accentuated her beautiful curves. She knew the sexy milf also appreciated how her young body looked all oiled up. Her choice of oil wrestling was partly to take away her oppoment's strength advantage, but mostly to make the wrestling match more sensual. Their slick skins would easily slide over each other, and the lack of grip would force them to grab each other wherever there would be any grip. She hoped for quite a few hand-on-thong grips during the fight.

Stacy enjoyed the feeling of the oil on her body. She made sure she covered every inch of it, to ensure her younger opponent would not have any grip advantage. When she was done, she tossed the empty bottle aside and sat down on her knees a few feet from the redhead. 'So, the first one to three pins wins?'

'I was thinking long control. Without a referee, we might argue whether a pin was scored. Control is much clearer. When you are in the top position, you have control. Your opponent must either get the top position or get back to her knees to break control. The one with control will slowly count to thirty to get a point. The first one to three points wins.'

Once again, Celeste had chosen rules which would make the wrestling match more sensual. The control rules would keep their bodies in close contact for long periods, giving lust time to grab hold of their souls before pulling them into its world of sexual pleasures.

'That sounds reasonable.' Stacy had been in long control matches before and knew just how horny these could make the contestants. There was always a lot a movement as the trapped wrestler tried to escape, causing thighs to rub over pussies and breasts to hug each other for prolonged periods. She was still confident she would beat the arrogant youngster, but she knew she would have lots of fun either way. Stacy's intention was still to have a competitive wrestling match with no sensual moves. However, she knew her opponent would try to turn her on during the match, but she was sure her wrestling skills would help her avoid getting too aroused.

'Let's fight for Julie's honour then.'

'I am ready when you are, young bitch.'

'I am always ready, old bitch.' Celeste knew this would rile up the older woman, who hated to be reminded of her age.

Both women slowly shuffled forward on their knees before grabbing hold of each other's necks. Their ample breasts smacked into each other as if high-fiving before their own personal battle. The two fighters strained against each other's bodies, trying to topple the other over. But both were fresh and full of energy, causing a stalemate, except for their breasts, which still smacked into each other with each sudden movement. Their nipples were rock hard, ready to joust whenever they got within range. They were only inches apart when the breasts hung in their natural position, but they met often when the breasts were activated by the movement of the two combatants' bodies.

'You are going down soon.' Celeste was determined to get the first point.

'I am too strong for you. After I've done toying with you, I will pin you.'

The women strained even harder, making their breasts smack into each other even more. It was only when Celeste pushed her knees too far back, and they slipped from under her, that they went down. The redhead reacted first and scramble to get on top of her opponent. Stacy twisted onto her back to have a better chance of fighting the young tigress off of her.

This allowed Celeste to get into a full body-to-body position. She had her friend's hands pinned next to her head, while her body lay flat on top of the brunette's body. Her breasts pinned their D-cup opponents flat against the milf's chest, while their nipples bend each other over in an equal struggle. Their flat tummies only had a thin layer of oil separating them, while their thighs pressed against each other's thong-clad pussies.

'You are failing Julie. I will soon fuck her brains out.' Celeste had used Julie only as an excuse to convince her older friend to wrestle her. The wrestling match had very little to do with the blonde. The redhead was not even sure she would pursue her the blonde should she win the wrestling match. But she thought that bringing Julie up every so often would make the brunette hot under the collar, as she truly kept her love life totally separate from her work life. She hoped this would distract the milf from focusing on the precious line she did not want to cross.

'You have not won the match yet, honey. You have not even won one pin yet.' Stacy saw through her sexy friend's plan. She knew she was using Julie to wind her up. Even though she was aware of what was going on, the mention of Julie's name still made her more determined to beat the redhead.

The two women kept struggling against each other. Every slight movement made their thighs glide over the other's stiff clit, waking up the lust-hungry she-wolves deep inside of them.

'One .. two.. three .. four.' The redhead counted slowly while struggling against every attempt of her stong opponent to roll them over. 'Fifteen .. sixteen .. seventeen.'

Stacy found it difficult to focus on getting on top. Her stiff clit was already buzzing with excitement from all the rubbing against the young woman's thigh.

She tried to move away, but her young friend's thigh kept finding her pussy, while the two women wrestled hard against each other.

'Auungghhhh.'

'Ahhhhhhhhhh.'

Both women moaned loud enough for the other to hear. The redhead did not hide her lust, but the brunette tried to make it sound like a grunt rather than a lusty moan.

Celeste knew she got slightly lucky to be in the top position, but she was willing to win the match any way she could. 'Twenty-two .. Twenty-three .. Twenty-four.' She lost control over the brunette's right hand, which did not bother her until she felt her thong being pulled upwards into a wedgie. The redhead forgot to continue with the count while fighting her opponent's hand to relief the pain from the thong biting into her bum and vagina. When this failed, she pulled the strings to undo the bows on either side of her hips. This caused the small thong to fly loose.

While the redhead focused on removing her own thong, Stacy suddenly twisted her body, rolling them onto their sides. She did not generate quite enough momentum to get on top, but she was no longer pinned down.

'Unggghhhhh. I thought you do not cross lines, bitch. Giving me a wedgie is pretty close to the line.'

'Ohhhhhhhhhhh. Wrestlers don't bitch and moan, honey.'

While the two women were on their sides, fighting to get on top, their pussies got a break from the constant thigh rubbing. This allowed Stacy to focus on the wrestling again. However, she was still filled with lust, and her pussy was yearning for more contact.

Celeste was also very aroused. She was disappointed at losing the initiative. While on top, she could ensure that her thigh rubbed her older friend's clit. Now, she had to focus on wrestling for position.

'Ohnnnggggg. You are too weak, bitch. I will soon have you pinned down.' Stacy suddenly shifted her body. Instead of trying to push the redhead onto her back, she pulled her while rolling over, trying to use her momentum to the sexy redhead over herself until she ended on top of the younger woman.

However, Celeste read the move and spread her legs, stopping the role as soon as she was on top of the brunette. 'Do you want to hand Julie's pussy to me on a platter now? That move may have worked when you were young, but it will never work with wrestlers of my generation.'

Stacy cursed herself for ending up on the bottom again. But when her opponent's pussy slid over hers, lusty thoughts replaced her thoughts about the bottom position. Her stiff clit was throbbing with joy almost immediately. She tried to twist her hips to break the contact, but this pushed her pussy tighter into her young friend's pussy.

Celeste was not about to let her opponent get out from under her again. She knew clit rubbing would distract the brunette, stopping her from launching another attack, so she made sure their lusty little buttons kept each other busy.

Stacy gasped with delight while their stiff clits dueled with each other. She knew she had to pull her pussy away from the redhead's pussy, but she could not get herself to do so. Instead, she pretended to struggle to get out of the hold, but she mainly used her efforts to bump and grind her pussy into its younger counterpart.

Celeste also pretended to move her hips, mainly to keep her opponent pinned down, but she carefully planned each movement to ensure their labia and clits rubbed into each other. However, she was getting much hotter with lust than she expected. Her lust was causing her to lose focus. She had to separate their pussies for a while to ensure she could execute her plan. She moved her leg between the older woman's legs and rested her thigh on the brunette's pussy to ensure she could still rub it without having to use her own pussy to do the job.

A few minutes later, Stacy was quickly losing her focus and control. Her lust was clouding her judgement, allowing her to move much closer to the forbidden line than she had planned to. She lifted her thigh until it pressed into her naked friend's pussy, before moving it about to rub her stiff clit. While doing this, she put in half an effort to topple the younger woman off of her, to make the rubbing look like an accidental touch while wrestling. She heard the redhead counting, but this was mere background noise, which did not really register with her.

'Oooohhhhhh. You have met your match, bitch. Do you want to give now, or shall I play with you a bit longer?' Celeste chose words which could be interpreted as her being dominant in a wrestling match, or her rubbing her thigh into her opponent's clit. She was caught in two minds. On the one hand, she wanted to let the round continue to make the brunette even hornier than she already was. On the other hand, she wanted to win the round, just in case she would like to pursue Julie in the future. Confident she could rub her friend's pussy again during the second round, she continued counting until she got to thirty.

The first point belonged to the younger woman, who was now even more self-assured than before the fight. The two fighters were breathing heavily when they got back to their knees. This was partly from the effort they'd put in wrestling each other, but mostly from being excited by all the clit rubbing.

'Are you going to put that back on?' Stacy pointed at the thong lying on the mat. She was hot with lust, but was comfortable that she was still in control of her desires. However, having rubbed her thigh and her pussy against her young friend's naked pussy while her own clit and labia had also been rubbed, brought her dangerously close to the edge. She hoped it would be easier to control her lust if the redhead's pussy was covered again.

'And give you another opportunity to give me a wedgie when I pin you down? No way. The thong stays off.' Celeste knew how horny her naked pussy had made the brunette and did not want to give up this advantage. She was sure the milf was very close to crossing the line, and she wanted to make sure she would not regain her composure to stop their flirting session again.

'I won't give you another wedgie.' Stacy was not comfortable wrestling the young woman while she was completely nude.

'I don't trust you. The thong stays off. You have yours on, so our pussies cannot accidentally touch each other anyway.'

The brunette was still not fully convinced, but her friend's argument made sense. 'You got lucky, bitch. You will not get lucky again.'

'One-nil to me, bitch. I can already feel Julie's pussy rubbing against mine.'

The mention of Julie made Stacy grab hold of her opponent to start the second round. This time, the brunette was more aggressive and toppled the sexy redhead over. Once on top, she easily controlled the younger woman. This time, her larger breasts pinned down their smaller, but firmer, opponents. The nipple contest was still even with neither set of nipples being able to bend the other all the way back. She kept her thighs away from her friend's pussy for now, but the redhead's pussy soon found her own pussy and started rubbing against it.

'Unggghhhhh. This will be where you spend the rest of the fight. You will never get close to Julie. I will make sure of that.'

'I will make Julie come from the bottom position. I can make anybody come from the bottom position.' Celeste rubbed her opponent's pussy harder and faster with her pussy to make her point.

'Ohhhhhhhhhh. You surely have much to say for somebody flat on her back.' Stacy's rock-hard clit was throbbing with delight, while rubbing faster into Celeste's swollen clit. The brunette's lust level was back to where it was at the end of the first round. She thought of pulling away from her opponent's pussy, but she could not show any weakness after the redhead's boast about being able to make anybody come from the bottom position.

Celeste did not want to stay at the bottom for too long. This would bring the round to an end too soon for her to really break down her older friend's sexual resistance. She considered returning the favour by giving the brunette a wedgie with her thong, but decided against it. For her plan to work, it was important that the milf became highly aroused, so she did not want to cause any pain to her pussy. Instead of pulling the thong upward, she pulled it down as far as she could.

When Stacy grabbed hold of her thong to pull it back up, the younger woman rolled them over. She quickly trapped her friend's legs between her own. This caused her naked pussy to rest on top of her opponent's thong-covered pussy for a few moments before their struggles forced her to lift her hips slightly.

The feeling of her young friend's naked pussy sliding hard over her own, almost drove Stacy over the edge. She had to concentrate hard to stop her from rolling her hips to grind her hungry pussy upwards. This felt like the natural thing to do, as she had done it so many times during previous sexfights. But instead, she mounted an all-out attack to roll them over. This failed, but caused their pussies to separate. However, their breasts were still in contact, but not pressed into each other as tightly as before. This slight separation allowed their nipples to glide over each other easier than before.

The joy from the nipple rubbing distracted the milf, but she recovered her focus again for another attempt to roll them over. As she thrusted upwards, their pussies made contact again. This time, she held her hips in position, allowing their pussies to kiss longer than before, albeit through the thin material of her small thong.

'Ohnnnggggg', Celeste moaned. 'I can make any woman come from the top position as well, bitch. Julie will beg me for mercy once I get on top of her.'

Celeste's body shook with lust. The pussy-to-pussy action made it difficult for her to focus on her plan. But she knew that their pussies kissing and slowly rubbing over each other would make the brunette extremely horny as well. She looked deep into the milf's eyes while rolling her hips to rub their clits harder over each other.

Stacy was too horny to respond. She did not want her opponent to realise that she was deliberately pushing her pussy upwards to press into the redhead's naked pussy. It had to look like an accidental touch because of hard wrestling. She therefore relaxed her hips and brought her bum down to the mat again, separating their pussies. As soon as the younger woman readjusted her body, she turned her body and rolled them over.

Celeste had been on top for a while and did not resist her older friend's attempt to roll them over. Her plan to make the round last longer than the previous one was working well. While their pussies were separated, she used the opportunity to grab hold of one of her opponent's breasts, squeezing it just hard enough to make the brunette moan with lust.

'Oooohhhhhhh. Let go, bitch, or I will maul your breasts as well.' The breasts grab was a surprise, but a pleasant one. In a competitive wrestling match, Stacy would not tolerate a blatant foul like this. But their wrestling match was no longer a competitive wrestling match. It had morphed into a sexual contest disguised as a competitive wrestling match. The breast grab was therefore par for the course and she knew her sexy young friend would not let go based on her threat. She gave the young woman only a few seconds before also grabbing hold of one of her breasts, and also squeezing just hard enough to cause pleasure.

'Mmmmmmmmmm. Julie will love it when I work her breasts. I bet she has long, sensitive nipples.' While saying this, Celeste trapped her opponent's stiff nipple between her index and middle fingers and pulled on it slightly. This brought another deep moan from the milf.

'Auungghhhh. You will never know what her breasts feel like or how sensitive her nipples are, honey.' The attention to her sensitive nipples drove Stacy wild with lust. She rolled them further until she ended up on top of the sexy young woman, ensuring that her thighs were outside the redhead's thighs. This allowed her pussy to rest on top of the hungry, naked pussy facing it. Not wanting to be too obvious, the brunette adjusted her body a few times, each time causing their stiff clits to duel through her thong.

Celeste had to fight her urge to come. The pussy rubbing was more intense now than before. She pressed her hips upwards to ensure their labia and clits could rub together often. While doing this, she looked deep into the brunette's eyes. She saw a raw lust which women only experience during a sexfight. Neither of them broke eye contact, while they rubbed pussies, pretending to wrestle.

Although her decision had been not to cross the line with her young friend, Stacy knew she had crossed the line already. The pussy-to-pussy rubbing was a few steps further than she had been prepared to go. Before the match had started, she had accepted that her best friend's daughter would try to cross the line, but she had not expected her own lust to force her to cross the line as well. Doubts set in. Should she stop the pussy contact, hoping that her opponent would think all the previous pussy rubbing she had started, was purely accidental?

Celeste was also having doubts. She was almost certain her mother' best friend was ready to go on a journey with her into the lusty world of competitive erotic contests. But she also wanted to make sure the option to pursue Julie later was open to her. This made her wonder whether she should go for another pin, or whether she should go all out to make her older friend as aroused as possible.

The young woman rolled them onto their sides, but the brunette did not allow her to get on top again. This forced the redhead to do something she knew would distract the milf. She grabbed hold of her thong, intending to rip it off. But when she felt the full pussy lips in her hand, she held onto them.

The pussy grab was exciting for a moment, but it also made Stacy realise they were way out of her comfort zone. She knew she had to stop the match before it went too far. But she also knew she was a pin down and that if she stopped now, her young friend would be the winner and would be free to go after Julie. Therefore, despite her reservations, the brunette continued wrestling. She mustered all her strength and rolled the redhead onto her back again, pinning her arms next to her head.

When the older woman began to count, Celeste pressed her thigh into her pussy and rubbed her clit and labia fast and hard, hoping to distract the brunette enough to roll them over again. But this time, Stacy held her focus, although her moans were loud and urgent. Her voice went husky with lust, but she kept naming the numbers, one after the other. Knowing she would soon lose the round, the young vixen continued rubbing her opponent's labia and clit. The closer the milf came to the count of thirty, the huskier her voice became and the more urgent her moans became.

The redhead was not too disappointed when the round was finally over. She had her older friend just where she wanted her, and she was sure the next round would be the one during which the brunette would finally be ready to cross the line.

'I am done, honey. This is getting out of control. It is time to go for a shower... in separate showers.'

'Why do you want to quit now? This is such a competitive wrestling match. The score is one each.'

'Our pussies keep grinding together. I am not comfortable with that.'

'It happens in most wrestling matches.' Celeste knew this was not accurate, but this made-up fact served her agenda. 'Just ignore it and focus on the wrestling. We are evenly matched. This is a great workout for both of us. I want to test myself against you. Don't you want the same?'

'How can I ignore the pussy rubbing? I think you may be doing it deliberately.'

'You are a sexfighter. My generation sexfighters know how to focus our minds away from the pleasure. Haven't your generation learned how to do the same?'

The young slut's arrogance pushed Stacy over the edge. She took her thong off and tossed it aside. 'Alright then, lets continue wrestling without thongs then, bitch. I will show you what my generation can do.'

A satisfied smile formed on Celeste's face. Her plan had worked. It was time to teach her older friend a sexfight lesson. 'I am ready, bitch.'

Chapter 9 – A Change of Weapons

The two sexy, oil covered bodies collided with a ferocity not seen during the first two rounds. The two fighters were fully aroused and ready to dominate the other sexually. This was still a wrestling match, but only in name. In reality, their weapons changed from strength and wrestling skills to lust and sexual prowess. Although their bodies would play an important supporting role, their lust-fueled pussies would wage the war between the two generations.

'I'm going to pin you so hard, bitch.' Stacy looked deep into her opponent's eyes, not trying to hide the lust in her voice. She held the younger woman tight against herself, not trying too hard to wrestle her down. Her whole body was crying out for close contact with the sexy, young body and she was giving it what it wanted.

'I will pin you right back, bitch. I will pin you like you've never been pinned before.' Celeste stared straight back into her friend's brown eyes. Her voice was also thick with lust. The feeling of the brunette's body pressed tightly into hers was extremely satisfying, for now. But her pussy demanded attention too. It needed contact with its rival and it was not willing to wait its turn.

'My generation wrestle in the nude when we want to show our inner strength as women.' Although she realised her daughter knew very well that baring her pussy was for a more erotic pussy-to-pussy sensation, Stacy still felt compelled to make an excuse for taking her thong off. Her stiff nipples sought out their jousting partners, immediately engaging in a sensual battle. Her clit reached out for its fellow duelist, but frustratingly could not reach it.

'My generation does not need an excuse to wrestle naked. We do it because we like it.' Celeste was tempted to kiss the older woman on the lips, but the time was just not right for that. This was still supposed to be a competitive wrestling match and an intimate act like kissing would reduce the mystique of the game they were now playing with each other.

'It sounds like a generation who needs to be taught a few wrestling lessons.' When Stacy saw the desire to kiss her in her young friend's eyes, she momentarily closed her eyes in anticipation of the sweet lips pressing against hers. But she quickly opened them again. Kissing was not on the menu yet.

Dessert always tasted better at the appropriate time. She intensified their breast and nipple battle to distract her from her desire to kiss the younger woman.

'Many women of your generation have tried to teach me wrestling lessons. All of them went home defeated but fully satisfied.' Celeste loved the sensual tango their breasts and nipples were dancing with each other, but it was time to invite their pussies to the dancefloor. She suddenly shifted her balance before driving her body forward and then twisting to her left.

The lusty milf did not expect the sudden attack and could not defend the takedown. The redhead quickly planted her knees between her opponent's inner thighs before forcing her legs apart. When she leaned forward to pin the brunette down, her naked pussy lay down on top of its equally naked opponent. Both women sighed deeply while looking deep into each other's eyes.

'Whore', moaned Stacy while her body shivered in anticipation of what was about to happen'

'Slut', replied the redhead. Her clit immediately found its rival while her moist labia kissed her friend's moist labia.

'Nggghhhhh. It's time for you to face the consequences of challenging me, tramp.' Although Stacy was on her back, with her breasts and pussy pinned down by her sexy young friend's breasts and pussy, she felt in control. In a competitive wrestling match, this would have been a bad spot to be in. But in a sexual contest between horny women, she was one of the best from her back. She brought her hips up, as if to throw her opponent off, but only managed to bump their pussies into each other. The pussy-to-pussy slap made her groan with lust.

'Ohhhhhhhhhhh. You are pinned down, tart. All of you are pinned down. From this position, I can do with you whatever I want to.' The pussy bump made the redhead bite her bottom lip with lust. She immediately retaliated by returning the pussy-to-pussy slap before grinding her moist labia and clit over the brunette's moist labia and stiff clit.

'Ohnnnggggg. You rely too much on your position, bitch. You will learn that a skilled fighter can use any position in a wrestling match to her advantage.' To make her point, Stacy moved again, this time ensuring her stiff clit glided directly over her young opponent's erect lust button. Her stiff nipples also found their jousting partners before pecking into them.

The two sexy, oil covered bodies glistened under the gym lights while sharing sexual bliss with each other. Neither woman would admit that they were deliberately grinding their clits and nipples into each other. Both still did this under the guise of a competitive wrestling match. Neither could hide their lust and neither was under any illusion that the other was actually still wrestling for pins.

'Auungghhhh. One.. Two.. Three.. Slut!' Celeste had no intention of counting all the way to thirty. She just wanted to remind her opponent that she was in control of the wrestling match and the pussy grinding. She bucked her hips with each count, sliding her labia over the brunette's labia.

'Aaaaahhhhhhh. Count this, whore.' Stacy shifted her body to the left, easily rolling them over, as there was little resistance from the redhead. Once on top, the brunette planted her knees between her opponent's legs before grabbing her arms and pinning them down. As she leaned forward, her pussy also pinned its opponent down

'Unggghhhhh. You won't be on top for long, bitch.' Celeste put in half an effort to wrestle her older friend off of her, but most of her focus was on lifting her hips to push her pussy tight into her opponent's pussy. Her body shivered when her lusty clit found the sexy milf's stiff clit.'

'Oooohhhhhhh. Now my whole body is pinning your whole body, slut.' Stacy's voice was thick with lust. Both of them knew exactly what she meant with 'my whole body'. The only portions of her body which was pinning anything down was her pussy, pinning its rival and her hands pinning her opponent's wrists to the ground. However, the brunette did not want to be the first to admit this was no longer a wrestling match, but rather a pussy brawl.

The two women were looking deep into each other's eyes while their most labia glided over each other. Their aroused clits were in a tense battle, sharing pleasure and lust as they rubbed into each other. Still, both women pretended they were in a competitive wrestling match. Celeste was comfortable with a pussy-to-pussy contest, but she was still scared her mother's best friend might stop the fight if she would call it a sexual contest or any other term with a sexual connotation. Stacy was still fighting an inner battle. She had crossed a line which she had never thought she would. This did not sit well with her, but her lust was ruling her body at the moment and would not allow her morals to interfere in its fun. The only way her brain could cope with the current situation was to pretend they were still wrestling, although she knew very well this was not the case.

'Mppphhhhh. Why are you panting so much, tart? Are you getting close to the edge..' Celeste paused before continuing, 'of your endurance?' The redhead knew her friend would understand exactly what she meant. She was also getting closer to the edge as a powerful orgasm stirred in her loins.

'Ahhhhhhhhhh. My endurance is just fine, bitch. But you seem to teeter on your endurance edge.' Stacy tried to hide how hard she had to fight her desires. Her nipples had been away from the action for a while, as she could not handle stimulation to them as well. But they were drawn to her young friend's lovely nipples, as if a strong magnetic field were pulling them in. Resistance was futile. The brunette slowly lowered her upper body until their breasts squashed together and their nipples pecked at each other.

'Unggghhhhh. I have outlasted many older women of your generation, whore. I will outlast you as well.' Celeste moved her upper body upwards until her firmer breasts flattened her opponent's larger breasts to make her point. She was getting close to the point of no return, but she was sure the lusty milf was even closer than she was. This drove her to go on an all-out attack, bucking her hips to drive her labia and clit over the brunette's pussy lips and sensitive love button.

'Auungghhhh. I have never met an arrogant young slut I could not beat in a .. wrestling match, tramp.' Stacy almost said 'sexfight', but caught herself just in time. Her focus was split between her breasts, pressing into the younger and firmer breasts, and her clit which was throbbing with pure pleasure. Losing focus while battling a building orgasm never ended well during a sexual contest. She had to break their pussy contact. Although she was on top, she suddenly threw her body to her left to roll them both onto their sides.

With their pussies separated, the women wrestled each other from their sides, neither trying too hard to get on top, but rather ensuring they would not end up on the bottom. Both needed their building orgasms to calm down before making pussy contact again. Although Celeste had been confident, she could make her older friend come before she would, she had been dangerously close to coming when the brunette had rolled them over to separate their pussies. She now knew she would have to be more careful when going pussy to pussy with the milf. Unlike the other older women she had beaten in sexfights, this one had stamina and lasting power. A sexfight against her would be a difficult and dangerous task.

The pussy fighting skills of her sexy young friend also surprised Stacy. Although there had been younger women who had pushed her to the edge during a sexfight, she had never been this close to coming before a younger woman did. She reassured herself that this was not a sexfight, and she was not truly in the right mindset to force the redhead to come before she did. But deep down, she knew the young woman would be a much tougher opponent than she had expected.

'What happened, slut? Did it become too hot for you on top of me?' Celeste was thankful for the reprieve. She was hoping to recover faster than her opponent to have an advantage when their pussies would clash again. She locked eyes with her friend and for a moment, her lips were drawn to the brunette's lips, but she restrained herself.

'I want to teach you a lesson before I pin you, whore.' Stacy knew what her opponent was referring to, but she steered away from talking about their pussy war. Looking into the redhead's eyes made it very difficult for her not to lock lips with her, but that would take away any pretense that this contest had not turned into a sexual contest. *'Not yet, at least'*, she thought, surprising herself for thinking that way.

'Oh, I think the old cat had learned a few new tricks tonight. You are the only one learning lessons, bitch.' Celeste feinted an attack to test her older friend's alertness. When the brunette wrestled back, she made sure she stayed on her side, without wasting too much energy. She was almost ready to challenge the milf's pussy with her own and was just waiting for an opening to earn the top position again.

'Experience come from learning during every fight, tart. If you don't learn, you will remain at the inexperienced level you are now.' Stacy knew this would get her young friend's back up and readied herself for another attempt to roll her onto her back. She was almost ready for another pussy duel, but she knew she had to be fully focused when crossing love swords with the younger woman again.

The wrestling match increased in intensity when Celeste reacted to her opponent's thinly veiled insult. Although she knew the milf only said this to get a reaction from her, she could not stop herself from reacting. The women were in a stalemate. Neither could turn the other onto her back. This frustrated the younger fighter, who desperately wanted to pin her older friend's pussy under hers, so she decided to employ dirty tactics. Grabbing hold of the brunette's left breasts, she gave it a hard squeeze. This made the milf yelp in surprise. When her hands came up to protect her breasts, the young woman suddenly exploded, easily turning her opponent onto her back.

'Bitch! Breast mauling is not allowed in a wrestling match.' Stacy was disappointed she ended up underneath the younger woman again. But she had little time to bitch about the rule breaking. The redhead's pussy was on top of hers again and her lust level jumped up the moment their clits met.

'Ahhhhhhhhhh. All is fair in love and brawls, slut.' Celeste's voice was low with lust, while she grinded her pussy into the brunette's pussy. This time she did not mask her pussy grinding as accidental rubbing during a wrestling match. She moved her hips while targeting her opponent's sensitive clit with her own.

'Ohnnnggggg. Two can play that game, whore.' Stacy grabbed hold of her young friend's neck and pulled her down while bringing her own upper body upward, slamming their breasts into each other. But instead of causing pain as she had planned, the breasts smacking into each other just turned both of them even more hot with lust.

'Mppphhhhh. It is time to finish you off, tramp,' moaned Celeste. Although her orgasm was quickly building up again, she continued grinding her wet labia and clit over the brunette's equally soaking wet labia and clit. Their breast battle was also in full force.

The redhead massaged her C-cups into the D-cups, while ensuring that their stiff nipples jousted as often as possible. The fight had changed in nature. There was an increased intensity and Celeste was no longer hiding the fact that this was a pussy brawl rather than a wrestling match. Stacy had not reached that point yet, but she did not complain about the increase in pussy-to-pussy action. She was fighting fire with fire, using her pussy as a lusty weapon.

'Ohhhhhhhhhhh. You are ready to surrender, bitch. I can see it in your eyes.' Celeste's voice was hoarse with pure lust. A very strong orgasm was building up fast. She was not sure how much longer her strong will could control it, but she kept grinding, hoping to make her opponent blink first.

'Oooohhhhhhh. I am just warming up, slut. I can wrestle for hours, can you?' Stacy's voice was croaky as she struggled to control her arousal levels. She was still not prepared to call the contest what it was. The orgasm stirring to life was quickly building up momentum and would soon be too mighty to control. The brunette still grinded her pussy upwards to meet her opponent's clit head-on with her own.

'Nggghhhhh. I never come first, whore. You will come before me.' Celeste was no longer beating around the bush. Their pussy war was about to end in a tremendous orgasm for one of them, and she was determined to be the one who lasted longer.

'Mmmmmmmmmmm. If you want a sexfight, I will give you a sexfight, bitch. Let's end this wrestling round and start the next round as a sexfight.' Stacy was very close to an orgasm and did not want to start the sexfight with an immediate orgasm. She was also too aroused to continue pretending they were still in a wrestling match.

'Aaaaahhhhhhh. I am glad you stopped pretending that we were wrestling, bitch. Our pussies have already started a duel.' Celeste was very excited that her mother's best friend had at last admitted her lust and had directly confirmed that the two of them would face each other in a sexfight. With a cheeky smile on her face, she continued. 'I was about to make you come, skank. But if you need a break, I will give you a break.' The redhead was also too close to the edge to continue without having a quick orgasm. Although she claimed the moral high ground, she needed the break as much as her older friend did.

Having brought each other to the brink of an orgasm, the women separated.

'I will fuck your brains out, bitch' Celeste looked deep into the brunette's eyes while saying this.

'In your dreams, whore.' Stacy returned the gaze, making sure her sexy young frienddid not see any weakness in her eyes.

After separating, the two women had some much needed water. Both were trying to lower their lust levels as much as possible before facing each other for the fourth round, when their pussies would continue their hostilities, this time with no pretence.

Chapter 10 – Pussy War

The two women glanced at each other while catching their breaths. Both were slightly flustered. They had a taste of the other's sexual prowess and knew they were in for a very tough sexfight. Although they could not wait to cross clits and nipples again, both had enough experience to know they needed recovery time before waging war against another highly skilled pussy fighter.

Both women knew their usual tactics might not work against the other. Stacy usually overwhelmed younger sexfighters, using her wrestling skills to pin them down before pleasuring them without a break. She found inexperienced fighters had to focus so much on fighting their own orgasms that they had no time to launch an attack on her clit or on her sensitive nipples. However, the redhead was also a good wrestler and had shown her she was more than capable of controlling her own lust while still driving her opponent wild with lust.

Celeste had never been afraid to go clit-to-clit with an opponent. Her strength during a sexfight was her ability to calm her orgasm down, while rubbing her clit over her opponent's clit at a frantic pace. This usually forced opponents to come before they had time to focus on controlling their lust. But her older friend had shown she could handle clit rubbing just as well as the redhead could.

'I have never lost a sexfight against a young, inexperienced sexfighter, like you. I've beaten them in one-round shootouts and in multiple rounds.'

'I have never lost a sexfight against an older woman without stamina, like you. I will make you come in every round of the match.'

'It is settled then. We fight three rounds.'

The two women were still more lusty than they wanted to be at the start of the sexfight, but both knew it was time to face each other in an erotic contest. Both wanted to face the other on equal footing to truly test their sexual skills.

They moved closer to each other until their sexy naked bodies pressed into each other. Feeling the other's soft skin against their own, hey looked deep into each other's eyes before their lips met for a tender kiss. Both women closed their eyes while slowly moving their upper bodies to massage their breasts into each other while their stiff nipples jousted with each other. They sucked on each other's lips for a while before both opened their mouths to allow their tongues to wrestle with each other.

The kiss turned from tender to passionate, driving both women wild with lust. Their tongues wrestled energetically before exploring each other's mouths. Soon, the women needed to feel the other's pussy against theirs. They broke the kiss and looked deep into each other's eyes.

Without having to discuss it, both women sat down, facing each other. Each lifted her right leg over the other's left leg and scooted forward until their pussies were merely inches apart. They took hold of the other's right wrists, while resting their left elbows on the mat for support.

'It is time for your sex education, honey.' Stacy looked deep into her younger friend's eyes while saying this. She moved her body slightly forward until their two wet pussies kissed, ready for combat.

'Sex has changed a lot since you last had any education, bitch. You have much to learn about the new techniques.' Celeste held her sexy older friend's gaze, seeing confidence, but knowing that the brunette was seeing the same in her eyes. The younger woman sighed loudly when their pussies pushed into each other. She immediately rolled her hips, driving her labia and clit over her opponent's labia and clit.

'Oooohhhhhhh. I've been wanting to teach you a sexfight lesson for a while now, young bitch.' The feeling of her opponent's smooth pussy lips kissing hers almost made Stacy forgot they were in a contest. But her competitive spirit soon kicked in. She slowly bucked her hips, making sure their labia pressed deep into each other, while their stiff clits engaged in a very sensual duel.

'Mmmmmmmmmm. I've wanted to sexfight you since the night we went skinny dipping in the lodge swimming pool during our last holiday together, slut.' Celeste's arousal levels went up while thinking of the night they were swimming completely naked, only meters away from where other holidaymakers were sleeping or making love. This caused her to increase the speed with which she grinded her pussy into her friend's pussy.

'Unggghhhhh. The way the moonlight made your naked skin glistened made me so horny, tart. I wanted to sexfight you there and then.' The image of her sexy friend's naked body in that swimming pool was still vivid in Stacy's mind. This made her body shiver with pure lust. The redhead's pussy grinding into hers also made her wild with lust. She bucked her hips faster to match the younger woman's rhythm, ensuring that their sensitive clits stayed in constant contact.

'Ahhhhhhhhhh. I was ready to beat you that night, just like I am about to beat you today, whore.' Celeste's muscles tensed with the thought of how a sexfight would have been that night. She bumped her pussy into the brunette's pussy, just hard enough to cause a jolt of pleasure in both their pussies.

With only a limited time to recover after their pussies had driven each other to the edge of an orgasm during the last wrestling round, the two women were already approaching the edge again. Both were confident of a win and both were determined to make the other come harder than she had ever come before. They therefore continuously attacked each other's clits, with little thought for defence.

'Mppphhhhh. The first time I took you to my self-defence class, your stiff nipples were clearly visible through your sweaty top. My nipples longed to joust with them. My clit longed to dominate yours, slut.' Stacy's voice was husky with lust. Her eyes looked deep into the younger woman's soul, while her clit continued duelling with its sensitive rival.

'Oooohhhhhhh. My nipples were only that hard from watching you wrestle. I wanted to wrestle you down and fuck you until you came, tart.' Celeste's voice was also low with lust. Her nipples were rock-hard and longing for contact with her sexy friend's hard nipples, but in their current position, this was not possible. She therefore focussed on their clit battle, while also ensuring that their moist labia glided over each other.

'Nggghhhhh. You will come for me soon, bitch. No young slut has a chance against my experience.' Stacy tightened her grip on the redhead's wrist, pulling her pussy tighter into the younger woman's soaking pussy while grinding faster and harder.

'Mmmmmmmmmm. Many older women have made the same promise to me, whore. All of them have begged me to stop while I made them come over and over again.' Celeste's body shivered with delight when her older friend intensified her attack on her pussy. This put her on the back foot for a moment, but she quickly fought back, driving her clit into the brunette's lusty sexfight sword.

'Aaaaahhhhhhh. Many arrogant young sluts have started with the same gusto you have started with, hussy. All of them have gone home disappointed, yet fully satisfied.' Stacy already had to fight her lust. The orgasm she had calmed down between rounds, were now wide awake again. Although her experience told her to protect her clit for a while, her pride forced her to continue sliding it over the younger woman's clit.

'Unggghhhhh. Many older sexfighters have made similar promises to me, slut. None of them could make good on those promises. Neither would you.' The orgasm which went to sleep earlier now opened up an eager eye. Celeste considered changing her tactics, but it was in her sexfighting DNA to go clit to clit with an opponent, and she would not change that against her friend.

Both women had to steel their minds to fight off the urge to succumb to their lust and allow the building orgasm freedom to take over their whole bodies. Both had the skills to take their clits away from the action for a while. However, neither wanted to show any weakness to the other by hiding their clits. They wanted not only to win. They wanted to send a message to the other. It was important for both to prove she was the sexfight queen of the family.

'Bitch!'

'Slut!'

'Auungghhhh. I can feel your pussy buzzing, whore. Don't fight it, come for me.' Stacy's voice was barely more than a whisper. Lust consumed her whole body, while her lust to win consumed her mind. She had to fight hard against her desires. An orgasm was quickly building up, and it was getting difficult to force it back. But she continued bucking her hips, grinding her labia and her clit urgently against the younger woman's soaking wet labia and clit.

'Ahhhhhhhhhh. I will never come before you, horny bitch. You may as well come now.' Her lust also made Celeste's voice low. With an orgasm building up, she was getting close to the edge. Although she had been there often before during sexfights, this time felt different. Her mind somehow was not as in control as before. She had to focus more than she was used to. Normally she was confident in a clit to clit battle, but doubt was quickly creeping into her mind. However, she continued grinding, not giving her opponent any respite.

'Ohnnnggggg. You do not have the skills to make me come, bitch. My experienced clit is schooling your puny clit.' Stacy looked deep into the redhead's eyes, trying to find weakness, but all she saw was a steely determination. This made her even more determined to beat the younger woman, although her body was already shivering in anticipation of the massive orgasm building up.

'Mppphhhhh. My clit has battled far more experienced clits than yours, slut. It tamed them all. It is busy taming yours.' Celeste saw just a slight hint of doubt in her older friend's eyes. She knew she was pushing the brunette further than she had ever been pushed, but she was also in uncharted waters. All she could hope for was that her opponent would surrender to her lust first.

'Ohhhhhhhhhhh. Your clit is buzzing like a vibrator with new batteries, bitch. You can't hide your lust from me.' Stacy grinded her pussy even faster over the redhead's pussy, hoping to push the younger woman over the edge. This brought her own body very close to the edge as well. Her orgasm was pushing hard against the dam wall, but she held the sluices closed, for now.

'Oooohhhhhhh. I can control my lust, slut. Your clit is buzzing as much as mine, and I know you won't be able to control your lust much longer.' Celeste also grinded faster to match her sexy older friend's rhythm. Her stiff clit was in a direct duel with the brunette's equally stiff clit. Although they were both buzzing with pure delight, both women kept their building orgasms under control.

With powerful orgasms building up in both women, they knew the end of the fight was close. Both believed it would be the other to surrender to the bliss of a mighty orgasm first. Their lusty moans were now louder than before, while they rubbed their pussies together as fast as they could.

'Nggghhhhh. I love you, but my pussy hates yours and will beat it up hard.' Stacy was now very close to an orgasm. She had to fight hard to keep it at bay. But she could feel her young friend's body trembling with excitement and knew she was very close as well, so she kept grinding her pussy into the redhead's pussy.

'Mmmmmmmmmm. I love you too, but my pussy will not take any abuse from yours. In fact, it will make yours cry very soon.' Celeste knew she could only fight her orgasm off for a short while. It was growing way too strong and there was only so much her mind could do to control it.

'Aaaaahhhhhhh. My pussy does not cry, slut. It makes other pussies, including yours, cry.' Stacy's voice was trembling with lust. She was balancing precariously on the edge, ready to lose control at any second. Only pride and determination to win made her hold on while her throbbing clit grinded over its sensitive rival.

'Unggghhhhh. My pussy ... Auungghhhh. No ... Nooo... Fuck Noooooooo!' Celeste could not believe she had lost control. Her whole body shook violently while a tremendous orgasm washed through it like a tsunami.

Auungghhhh. Yes, fuck me slut. Fuck me hard!' The moment she felt her opponent's orgasm, Stacy stopped fighting her desires. 'Ohhhhhhhhhhh. Make me come, slut! Aaaaahhhhhhh. Yes. Oh fuck, yes. Ohnnnggggg . Yes, yeesss, yeeessss!' She kept grinding until her own body was rocked by a mighty orgasm about ten seconds after the redhead succumbed to her lust.

After riding out her orgasm, the brunette pulled the younger woman towards her and gave her a tender kiss on the lips. 'You've put up a good fight, but my experience is just too much for you.'

'We will see in the second round.' Celeste was still very disappointed and not in a talkative mood.'

Chapter 11 – Tongues versus Clits

Stacy felt more confident after winning the first sexfight round, but she knew it had been too close for comfort. She glanced over at her disappointed friend, seeing a mixture of frustration and determination in her eyes. The brunette knew she was in for an even tougher round than the first. She started the second round before the younger woman had much time to fully recover mentally from the first-round defeat.

'Are you sure you want to try again, honey? I don't want to destroy your confidence as a sexfighter.'

'You got lucky in the first round. You will not get lucky again, bitch.'

The two women walked towards each other, hugging tightly before kissing each other on the mouth. Their breasts squeezed deep into each other, while their stiff nipples pecked at each other. This time, the kiss turned passionate almost immediately. Their tongues wrestled aggressively, while they held the back of each other's heads to keep their faces close.

While they continued kissing, Celeste lowered her right hand until it found her older friend's wet pussy. Her fingers slowly slid up the labia until it found the brunette's vagina. She slid her middle finger into the moist hole at the same time she slid her tongue into her opponent's mouth.

Stacy gasped with delight before her fingers quickly found the redhead's pussy. With her own pussy being pounded fast, she did not waste time before sliding her middle and index fingers into the redhead's vagina.

The kiss the women shared intensified in passion while they fingered each other hard. They were both moaning loudly when Celeste broke their kiss. Her lips sought out the brunette's slender neck, kissing it deeply before nibbling on it just hard enough to make the hot milf shiver with delight.

Stacy immediately moved her lips to her young opponent's neck as well, but she felt she was one step behind the younger woman, so she wrestled her down. Once they were both on the mat, the brunette placed her knees above her the redhead's head. Once in place, she lowered her breasts over the redhead's face, while sucking on the younger woman's nipples and breasts. The nipple 69 soon had both women moaning with lust.

Celeste knew she had a disadvantage as she regularly had nipple orgasms. Her older friend was expertly sucking on her left nipple while gently stroking the other with her fingers. This made a powerful orgasm stir up. Not knowing whether the brunette could also come from nipple play, she decided to take control over the fight. She grabbed hold of the milf and rolled them over. Once on top, she moved her body until her mouth was over the brunette's pussy.

Stacy's body tensed up when her young friend kissed her pussy lips. She immediately lifted her head and licked the redhead's labia before her tongue found her stiff clit. She flicked the little button as fast as she can while kissing it in between.

The two women licked, sucked and kissed each other's clits fast and passionately, driving the other to an ecstasy level where neither could control their lust. Both were soon ready to come, fighting a losing battle against their desires. Stacy's mind was strong, but her lust was stronger. She held out as long as she could, while her tongue worked her young friend's clit, but it was only a question of time before a mighty orgasm exploded through her body.

Celeste kept her pussy on top of the brunette's mouth, until the older woman's tongue forced an orgasm out of her as well, a few seconds after she had forced the milf to come. Both women lay back on the mat, allowing all the aftershocks to wash through their bodies.

'I told you that you got lucky in the first round.' Celeste squeezed her opponent's breast while saying this.

'Your tongue may have beaten my pussy, but my pussy has still tamed yours. I am still the pussy fighting queen.' Stacy allowed her young friend to massage her breast, while she recovered for the all important third round.

Chapter 12 – The Pussy Fighting Queen

After resting for a while to fully recover from their second orgasms, Celeste got back to her feet. 'I am ready, bitch. Do you want to give up now or should my pussy teach yours a lesson it will never forget?'

'My pussy has been gentle with your pussy before. This round, it will be a no-rules brawl to the end.'

'Your clit will face the champion clit, bitch.'

'My mighty clit will introduce your puny clit to the big leagues this round, slut.' Stacy also got back to her feet and immediately grabbed hold of her sexy friend, trying to wrestle her down.

'I am the better wrestler and the better sexfighter, whore. You will soon be on your back coming all over the place.' Celeste wrestled back, grabbing hold of the older woman's hair and pulling on it while trying to topple the brunette over.

'Your arrogance will come back to bite you, tart.' Stacy suddenly stepped to her right, twisting her body. This pulled the redhead off balance, causing her to tumble to the mat with the brunette falling on top of her.

The sexfighting milf grabbed hold of both the younger woman's wrists and pinned them next to her head. She forced her knees between the redhead's thighs before laying down on top of her, pressing their wet pussies and their large breasts into each other.

After unsuccessfully trying to bump her sexy older friend off of her, Celeste wrapped her legs around the brunette's body, pulling their pussies even tighter together. She rolled her hips, driving her clit into the milf's stiff clit.

'Ohnnnggggg. My pussy does not like arrogant pussies. It will make your pussy beg for mercy, bitch.' It surprised Stacy how fast her opponent's clit was exciting hers. Although she had the top position, the redhead was dictating the pace. The brunette bucked her hips, trying to wrestle back control over the pussy war. Her labia slid over their smooth opponents while her clit did direct battle with its rival.

'Ahhhhhhhhhh. Your pussy is upset because it met its match, tramp. It will soon admit defeat.' Celeste's voice was dripping with lust. She preferred to be on top in order to control the contest, but she had a few tricks from the bottom position as well. To disrupt her older firend's rhythm, she bumped her pussy upwards a few times, before rubbing her clit over the brunette's clit, setting the rhythm she wanted to fight at.

'Auungghhhh. My pussy will never surrender to yours, tramp.' The two pussy bumps made Stacy moan loudly with pure lust and broke the rhythm with which she had grinded the youger fighter's clit. Her own clit was now under attack, and her orgasm was quickly building up. She had to get it out of the action for a while to refocus. While still pinning the redhead down, she adjusted her body until her labia rubbed over the younger woman's clit, giving her own clit a break from the action.

'Unggghhhhh. Your cowardly clit is already hiding from my superior clit, whore. Is it afraid to duel?' Celeste was quickly moving towards another orgasm. With her clit being the only one getting attention, she tried to move her body to ensure a clit-to-clit battle. But the older woman trapped her too tightly. Her only option was to go after the milf's sensitive nipples. She rolled her shoulders to find the older woman's stiff nipples with her own, jousting with them while their breasts massaged each other.

'Aaaaahhhhhhh. My clit is exactly where I want it to be, and so is your clit, bitch.' Stacy had more control over her lust with her clit being mostly out of the action, but the attention to her nipples was slowly building up her orgasm again. She continued attacking the younger woman's clit with her labia, confident this would force the redhead to come soon.

'Mmmmmmmmm. There are more ways to make you come, slut.' Celeste's voice was low with lust. She knew she was in trouble, but she had been in this position before and had always found a way out. She continued pecking at her opponent's nipples with her own, before lifting her head and kissing the brunette on the lips. After sucking on her lips for a few seconds, she forced her lips open with her tongue to challenge the milf's tongue to a wrestling match.

The two women kissed each other passionately while their nipples jousted in a sensual duel. Their loud, lusty moans were filling the room, while a layer of sweat covered their sexy bodies. Stacy remained in control and was still rubbing the younger woman's clit with her labia. It seemed to be just a matter of time before she would force another orgasm from the redhead. But Celeste could take a lot of attention to her clit before her mind lost control over her desires.

She was determined to win and would do whatever it took to stop herself from coming before she could get the brunette to have a massive orgasm.

'Unggghhhhh. I will allow you to eat out my pussy if you come now, slut,' whispered Stacy, after breaking their kiss for a moment. The nipple war forced her much closer to the edge than she wanted to be. But she was still very confident that she would beat the younger woman as long as she could keep her pinned down. Her labia mercilessly drove pleasure and lust into the redhead's stiff clit, while she looked deep into her friend's eyes.

'Aaaaahhhhhhh. Your pussy would be too sensitive after I make you come, bitch. You could not handle my tongue flicking your clit.' Celeste forced her tongue into her older friend's mouth after saying this. Her clit was buzzing with lust and a mighty orgasm was fighting her mind for control. Although her nipples were forcing the milf towards the edge through her sensitive nipples, she knew she was losing the battle of lust.

'Nggghhhhh. Your tongue is skillful. I will give you that, tart. But it will play no role in this round.' Stacy's voice was laced with lust. She could not believe how much the nipple play and her labia gliding over the younger woman's clit aroused her. Although she still felt in control, she increased the speed with which she attacked to redhead's buzzing clit, before locking lips with her again.

'Ohhhhhhhhhhh, I have many skillful sexfighting weapons, whore. You will soon taste all of them.' Instead of locking lips with her opponent again, Celeste move her head until her lips found the brunette's neck, just under her ear. The first few kisses brought deep moans from the milf, but when she sensually nibbled on the slender neck, she knew she had discovered another weak spot in her opponent's armour. She continued kissing and nibbling on the sensitive neck while her nipples kept jousting with their sensitive opponents.

'Ohnnngggggg. The only effective sexfight weapons are mine, bitch.' Stacy grinded her young friend's stiff clit even faster and harder to make her point. Her nipples were throbbing with desire while her body shivered every time the redhead nibbled on her neck. This was all distracting her, making it difficult to focus on controlling her lust. It also made her lose her grinding rhythm slightly, but she kept attacking the younger woman's clit as best she could.

'Auungghhhh. Your only weapon is failing against my mighty clit, tramp.' The erratic rhythm with which her older friend attacked her clit reduced the constant pleasure her clit had been exposed to. This gave the younger woman an opportunity to focus more on her offence. She nibbled the milf's sensitive neck slightly more aggressively. When she felt the brunette was distracted, she kicked her hips upwards while twisting her body.

This caught Stacy by total surprise. By the time she tried to shift her weight, it was too late. She was on her back with her opponent pinning her down. The brunette fought hard to turn them over again, but the younger woman kept her balance and stayed on top. When the milf got too tired to buck her body, the redhead placed her right knee between the older woman's thighs and her left next to her right thigh. She grabbed hold of Stacy's left leg and lifted it to her shoulder before lowering her hungry pussy onto the brunette's soaking wet clam.

'Aaaaahhhhhhh. The tide has turned, slut. It is time for your clit to join the battle.' Celeste's voice was full of triumph and determination. She knew the fight was hers to win, and she was not about to let her opponent gain control again. The redhead immediately targeted the milf's clit with her own love button, grinding fast while looking deep into the brunette's eyes.

'Nggghhhhh. The tide is still flooding towards you, just like your orgasm will flood your pussy soon, bitch.' Stacy's orgasm, which had been building up slowly, was now rushing towards the edge because of the attention to her clit. The only way she could win this round was to go on the attack, so she bucked her hips upwards, driving her clit over the younger woman's stiff clit.

'Ohhhhhhhhhhh. Your clit is like a small boat caught in a big storm, whore. It is just a matter of time before the waves of lust swallow it in.' Celeste's voice was hoarse with lust. Her orgasm was still building quickly, and she did not know how long she could still control it. She considered taking her clit out of the action, but after she had talked trash to her older friend for doing that, she could not do it herself. It was a clit-to-clit shootout and all she could hope for was to outlast her experienced opponent.

'Ohnnnggggg. My clit has been through mighty storms, floozy. It is not afraid of the ripple you are making in the pool.' Although her words were combative, Stacy's voice gave away just how close she was to an orgasm. It was trembling and full of doubt. The brunette was fighting her urges with all she had, but the orgasm was just too strong and she had great difficulty in holding it back. Her hips were still bucking to drive her clit into the redhead's clit, but this was more through instinct than by design.

'Auungghhhh. Your clit is clearly drowning in lust, slut. Save it, come for me.' Celeste's voice was trembling just as much as her sexy friend's voice. Her clit was buzzing with pure delight, while a wild orgasm was pushing hard against the door, trying to force it open. She was about to come again and her mind knew it lost the battle, but she kept grinding her clit into her opponent's clit while looking deep into the brunette's eyes.

'Aaaaahhhhhhhh... Bitch! .. You fucking bitch! Nggghhhhh. No, I can't .. Ohnnnggggg. Noooo! Fuck! Noooooo!' Stacy lost the battle against her lust. Her body shook wildly as an enormous orgasm rocked it over and over again.

'Unggghhhhh. Come for me, bitch, come for me like the slut you are.' Celeste kept grinding her hungry clit over the brunette's throbbing clit, now working on her own orgasm, while looking deep into her defeated opponent's eyes. 'Mppphhhhh. Right there, whore, grind faster. Mmmmmmmmmm. Oh yes. Fucking yeesss, yeeessss, yeeeesssss! About thirty seconds after forcing an orgasm from the older woman, Celeste surrendered to her urges as well.

A huge orgasm turned her legs into jelly forcing her to slump down next to her friend. The two women lay next to each other in silence with very different emotions. The redhead was delighted and proud of her win. Stacy was very disappointed, but still proud of the younger woman for being able to push her over the edge.

'You beat me fair and square, but I will not let that happen again. Next time I will make you come until you are too exhausted to get up.'

'I can't wait to make you come again. But I need a day to recover. I am sure you do too.'

The two women leaned over to give each other a tight hug and a caring kiss on the lips.

'I love you, honey.'

'I love you too.'

Both knew just how much they cared for each other, but both also knew they would be ruthless competitors during future sexfights.

That night, while getting ready for bed, Stacy opened her diary to a blank page. She thought for a few moments before making an entry.

'It finally happened. An arrogant young slut has beaten me in a sexfight today. It was a narrow defeat, but I still lost. I hereby vow that this will never happen again. I will never lose to today's opponent or any other arrogant young slut ever again.'

In her room, Celeste opened a diary app on her tablet. After naming the entry *'A Tough Test'* her fingers started typing.

'I had a sexfight today. This was not my first sexfight, not by far. But it was one of my toughest and most rewarding sexfights. I beat a very skilled older sexfighter. She pushed me further than I thought I could ever go. I want to .. scratch that. I need to face her again. I need to know that this was not an off day for her or just luck on my side, I need to beat her again to know I am the better sexfighter.'

The End

Don't miss out!

Visit the website below and you can sign up to receive emails whenever Ian Faber publishes a new book. There's no charge and no obligation.

https://books2read.com/r/B-A-UYSW-HXZFC

BOOKS 2 READ

Connecting independent readers to independent writers.

Did you love *Sexfight Diary*? Then you should read *Workplace Sexfights*[1] by Ian Faber!

After sexfighting each other during a trip to a small town, Vivian and Gwen had regular sexfights against each other. Soon, they found that many other women enjoyed to compete in this most erotic of contests.

With sexfighters looking for a contest, the workplace became a lot more interesting than it used to be.

1. https://books2read.com/u/b5qJw6

2. https://books2read.com/u/b5qJw6

Also by Ian Faber

17th Century Sexfighters
A Dangerous Journey
Friendships Rekindled
The Female Island
True Freedom

21st Century Sexfighters
Porn Stars Reading Lines
Popular Porn Stars

Erotic Combat World Championship
Erika's First Sexfight
Ulrike, the Sexfighting Student

Good Friends, Better Lover
A New Opportunity
Workplace Sexfights

Standalone

Sexfight Diary

Ingram Content Group UK Ltd.
Milton Keynes UK
UKHW040704200323
418846UK00001B/74

9 798215 089231